Ciicothe's Seven Rivers

(Ciicothe's Neeswathway Theepay)

*To: Mike
Thanks*

J.R. Johnson

Copyright © 2017 J.R. Johnson.

All rights reserved. No part of this book may be reproduced, stored, or transmitted by any means—whether auditory, graphic, mechanical, or electronic—without written permission of the author, except in the case of brief excerpts used in critical articles and reviews. Unauthorized reproduction of any part of this work is illegal and is punishable by law.

ISBN: 978-1-4834-6841-9 (sc)
ISBN: 978-1-4834-6842-6 (e)

Library of Congress Control Number: 2017905811

Because of the dynamic nature of the Internet, any web addresses or links contained in this book may have changed since publication and may no longer be valid. The views expressed in this work are solely those of the author and do not necessarily reflect the views of the publisher, and the publisher hereby disclaims any responsibility for them.

Any people depicted in stock imagery provided by Thinkstock are models, and such images are being used for illustrative purposes only.
Certain stock imagery © Thinkstock.

Lulu Publishing Services rev. date: 5/15/2017

Dedication

In memory of Karen Sue "Susie" Johnson

I dedicate this story to the strong women in my life and the powerful influence they had in molding me into a man, sharing their wisdom and knowledge of our family history with me. It is no fault of theirs how I distorted our history to spin this tale.

I go to bed with a turd behind each ear and get up in the morning knowing the smell of shit!

- Grandma Lulu Golden

I have for many years past, contemplated the noble races of red men, who are now spread over these trackless forests and boundless prairies, melting away at the approach of civilization. Their rights invaded, their morals corrupted, their lands wrenched from them, their customs changed, and therefore lost to the world; and they at last sunk into the earth, and the ploughshare turning the sod over their graves---millions of whom have fallen victim to the smallpox and the remainder to the sword, the bayonet, and whiskey; all of which means of their destruction have been introduced and visited upon them by acquisitive white men---yet phoenix-like they may rise from the stain of the painter's palette and live again upon canvas, and stand forth for centuries yet to come, the living monuments of a noble race.

- George Catlin 1832

Live in perpetual peace with the Indians…cultivate an affectionate attachment from them…The decrease of game rendering their subsistence by hunting insufficient we wish to draw them to agriculture, spinning and weaving…When they withdraw themselves to a small piece of land, they will perceive how useless to them are their extensive lands and forests and will be willing to pare them off…in exchange for necessaries…We shall push our trading houses they will be glad to see the good and influential individuals among them (the Indians) will run into debt…When these debts get beyond what the individuals can pay, they become willing to lop them off…by a cession of their land.

Marked: Private and unofficial, To Governor Northwest Territory
- Letter to: William Henry Harrison
From: President Thomas Jefferson, Nov. 1802

The only good Indian is a dead Indian.
The Indian Savages could replace the black slaves or be eliminated.
- President Andrew Jackson, Sept. 1833

Conquest is not only a right but a duty.
I will rid Germany and the world of Jews.
- The Fuehrer Adolph Hitler, Sept.1933

Your Great White Father! The President of the United States.
- William Henry Harrison, Aug. 1810

My Father? - The sun is my father, the earth is my mother - and on her bosom, I will recline.
- Tecumseh, Aug. 1810

In our intercourse with our aboriginal neighbors, the same liberality and justice which marked the course prescribed to me by two of my illustrious predecessors when acting under their direction in the discharge of the duties of superintendent and commissioner shall be strictly observed. I can conceive of no more sublime spectacle, none more likely to propitiate an impartial and common creator, than a rigid adherence to the principles of justice on the part of a powerful nation in its transactions with a weaker and uncivilized people whom circumstances have placed at its disposal.
- William Henry Harrison, Inaugural comments concerning Indians' fate. March 4, 1841

Contents

Acknowledgements xiii
Prologue xv

Chapter 1 1
Frog Town   April 1963   on the Ohio

Chapter 2 9
Prophetstown   November 1811   on the Tippecanoe

Chapter 3 21
Terre Haute   1811-1813   on the Wabash

Chapter 4 29
Vincennes   1813-1814   on the Wabash

Chapter 5 37
North Bend   1814-1822   on the Great Miami

Chapter 6 51
Frog Town   May 1963   on the Ohio

Chapter 7 55
The Underground Railroad   1822-1823   on the Scioto River

Chapter 8. 63
The General Store Secrets   South Point   1824-1829   on the Ohio

Chapter 9. 73
Tecumseh's Curse   1830-1834   on the Ohio

Chapter 10. 79
The Lost Cherokee   1835-1838   on the Ohio

Chapter 11. 85
Dripping Beaver at the Cold Wave   July 1963   Ironton on the Ohio

Chapter 12. 89
The Devil's Election   1839-1840   on the Ohio

Chapter 13. 97
Finding Tecumseh   August 1963   South Point on the Ohio

Chapter 14. 103
Eli's Coming   Winter 1840-1841   Cincinnati on the Ohio

Chapter 15. 107
Lumpkin's Jail   February 1841   on the Potomac

Chapter 16. 111
The Poor House and Woodland Cemetery   August 1963   Ironton on the Ohio

Chapter 17. 117
The Great White Father's Inaugural   March 1841   Washington on the Potomac

Chapter 18. 125
Greasing the Wheels of the Presidential Coach to Hell   April 1841   Washington on the Potomac

Chapter 19 133
Two Funerals   September 1963   Ironton on the Ohio

Chapter 20 139
The Journey Home   May 1841   South Point and North Bend on the Ohio

Chapter 21 143
Trouble Comes in Pairs   September 1841   on the Ohio

Chapter 22 147
The Ghost of Willow Wood   May 1964   on the Ohio

Chapter 23 153
The Protector of the Bones   September 1964   Ironton on the Ohio

Chapter 24 161
Will the Last Indian to Depart Ohio Turn off the Lights   1843   Cincinnati on the Ohio

Chapter 25 165
In the Tears of God   1843-1844   South Point on the Ohio

Chapter 26 171
Grandma Lu Goes Old School Prophet   November 1964   Ironton on the Ohio

Epilogue 179
The Ghost of Time

Acknowledgements

Thanks to God and Jesus Christ foremost in my life.

I would like to give thanks to the people that played a significant part of making this book possible:

My Grandmas, for their love and inspiration. I know they are in a forest in Heaven collecting roots and herbs for the Great Good Spirit, God!

My Mother, for her quiet love and dedication to fourteen children, a tribe of no regrets.

Frank "Bubby" and Mike "Wiggy" Johnson, for their contributions to this story.

Ike and Edna Meeks, who treated me as a son.

My son Jimmy, for his love and tech support, without it this story could not be told.

My love Jody, who saved my life, without her I would not exist. I thank her for getting me off my butt and back to work on completing this book. She brought the light of love back to my life. She is my inspiration for living. I am blessed to have an angel on each side of the circle of life.

Joseph, for his input and inspiration to complete this book.

My friends Greg and Karen, for their support, love, and allowing me to twist some of their family's history as if it were my own.

The Four Winds Cherokee Tribe of Louisiana, for the Pow-Wow that awoke me from a long sleep.

My friends and family members, for their feedback and listening to my bull for years.

Sherman Alexie, author of *The Absolutely True Diary of a Part-Time Indian*, for the nudge in the right direction.

The Alabama-Coushatta Tribe and Tigua Tribes of Texas, who inspired me through their ongoing fight for their tribal rights.

The Ohio Historical Society, for the eye-opening tour of the Moravian settlement of Schoenbrunn and the Delaware Christian Indian massacre site at Gnadenhutten on the Tuscarawas River. Thank you for not hiding the evil past.

Prologue

Life is tough when you are poor. We were the poorest family in Lawrence County, Ohio. Heck, maybe even the poorest family in the state or country! It's tougher still when you find out that you are a poor-ass, half-breed Indian with no reservation or tribal support, whose great-great-great-grandmother may have pulled off the first assassination of a president! This story would take courage to tell.

Nothing I learned about my Indian heritage or this evil president during the hot summer of 1963 gave me cause to be ashamed. Fear of retaliation from this evil man long in the grave was my greatest concern. After one hundred twenty years (when this story is revealed), maybe people could accept the truth.

But perhaps two hundred years was needed to heal the deep wounds inflicted by the overpowering greed of people who professed to be good Christians. My Great-Grandmother Wick always said that these so-called Christians only prayed with their mouths, never with their hearts.

As you read this story, you will see that my grandmothers had numerous prophetic sayings. Some intended to help, others were meant to cut you to the bone. My grandmother and great-grandmother lived together in a small, wood-framed, shotgun-style house in Ironton, Ohio.

Ironton is a city in the southern section of the state that overlooks the Ohio River. It is known for the iron and coal resources provided for the Union during the Civil War. It is also known for its hard-nosed Fighting Tiger High School football, the Ironton Tanks (a defunct semi-pro football team of the 1920's), and its strong, hillbilly spirit.

My great-grandmother, Grandma Wick, was born on my birthday (day and month) in 1872, which gave us somewhat of a blood bond. She was born under the veil (a membrane over the face at birth said to have some mystic value), as was I. My grandmother, Grandma Lu, was born on January 1, 1900.

My grandmas were widows who lived independently and used the gathering of native herbs and roots for the making of Indian medicines to supplement their income. Their spring elixir, cold and flu remedies, poultices, snake oil, itch cream, bug repellant, and all the other concoctions that they used for diseases or problematic injuries were widely known. They were also used by a varied range of the population of Ironton, Lawrence, and Scioto Counties in Ohio.

The education of the Shawnee Indian medicine trade was passed on to my Grandma Wick from her Grandma Willow (Ciicothe) Reed, who died in 1905. She was either one hundred four or one hundred five years old. No one was sure of her correct age. She died while on an outing to collect medicine plants and roots, a task she truly loved. Her tote was full of snakeroot, willow bark, ginseng root, sassafras, various tree bark, May apple, buckeyes, tickseeds, and hemp plant. Heck! I know how she died, she was loaded like a pack mule and broke her back!

My old daddy always called my grandmas old, crazy Indian witches and said the brews they made were just poisons. This was most likely the kindest thing he would say concerning my grandmas; for example, he always referred to them as Black Dutch or nigger Indians. So it should be no surprise that my old man made threats to kill my grandmas during any one of his numerous drunken stupors.

I can only guess why daddy hated my grandmas. Maybe it was because when he put a beating on my mom or the rest of us young ones that our grandmas were always there as our safety net. Our angels didn't work with his plans. Mom would move in with the grandmas until the old man came around sweet talking her into coming home. It seemed as if dad's master plan was to keep mom pregnant. By 1963, I had seven brothers and five sisters. His plan appeared to be working. The grandmas' house was not big enough to stack this half-breed tribe in all its corners, so there were times we had to live on the streets.

Now you might say my daddy was mean. Yes, he was, stand by for a good butt-kicking when the Miller was flowing. The old man had his problems; we often tried to guess the cause. He was a decorated, wounded World War II veteran who always worked hard to provide for us, but as our family grew bigger, it became poorer. The old man became more frustrated, more mean, and more inclined to the bottle.

I often wished that I was an only child, things might have been different. Maybe just my older brother Bubby, my older sister Sharon, and I would have been the extent of our family, but who of the remainder of the tribe would I wish away? I loved all of my younger brothers and sisters.

My daddy had his opportunities to be a success. His father died in 1950 and had acreage with good farmland at Myrtle Ridge, Ohio. My dear dad decided not to pay the tax debt and lost the chance to go back to the farm where he was raised. Heck, a very smart man once said that the First National Bank of Ironton could not provide for the tribe that the old man was trying to raise.

Daddy told us his great-great-great-grandfather, who came from North Carolina in the early 1800's, was distant kin to President Andrew Johnson. But that story is a wild one and will have to be told another time.

I guess it was fortunate that I made that ill-fated trip to the Ironton Beachwood Park sand pit with my best friend, Magoo. If you can call all that pain from a busted scrotum sack, broken bones, and a damaged knee fortunate. I broke my body up, which killed my incredible speed. My busted knee destroyed my dream of playing college football at Ohio State.

Oh, yes, I was fast! When the old man would take me hunting for rabbits, he used me like a good beagle dog. I would flush rabbits out from the farm fields. Running alongside the rabbits, I would reach down to check and see if they were big, fat ones or little, skinny ones. The signal from me to my dad was one finger up for skinny, two fingers up for fat. If I held up two fingers, then I had to turn on the burners in order to outrun the bullet. You see, the old man hated to waste a good bullet on a skinny old rabbit.

Ironton, Ohio is a town populated by approximately fifteen thousand people. Located on the banks of the Ohio River, the industry is diverse with coal and iron leading the way. Most of my family made their livings at the Dayton Malleable Iron Foundry. My daddy bucked the family tradition by driving a long-haul truck (eighteen wheeler). Steel, iron casting, and new cars were just a few of the things he hauled.

He was currently hauling big rig truckloads of Miller High Life beer from Milwaukee to Sprigs Distributing Company in Ironton, Ohio. You might have known he would find his dream job. His motto was, "Drink all you can, deliver the rest." I made one trip to Milwaukee with him in 1960, and that was enough for me. I could see his job was part of his personal hell.

Indian history, legends, and stories are passed on by word of mouth. Rarely is it accurately recounted by white historians. White man's version of history is, in most cases, developed to change events. It permits the haze of time to cover up or whitewash events of the hell and devastation leveled on a good people that only wanted to live in their homelands and prosper with their families.

I believe that if I had not injured myself on that April morning in that last dumb-ass jump of the day into that cursed Beachwood Park sand pit, I would not have slowed my running around like a one-winged fly long enough to listen to my Grandma Wick's story. She had told stories about our Indian heritage in the past, but I was too full of myself to give her stories the attention they deserved. So I am going to lay back and listen to my old grandma spin this tale while I try to recover from my nosedive into the God-forsaken sand pit. Hopefully, I can get put back together with my grandma's ancient Indian healing remedies.

With all the years it took me to put this story on paper, the haze of time has taken (through death) all the people that had lived this nightmare. Somehow, the story survived to allow me to sieve through most of the facts. I was forced to fill in the blanks, which compels me to call this a work of fiction.

It's time for Grandma Wick to fire up the old, stone, Indian smoking pipe with a bowlful of kinnikinnick and begin to tell this most unbelievable story.

CHAPTER 1

Frog Town   April 1963   on the Ohio

I have paid little or no attention to the fact that you should always listen to the little voice in your head. On this warm, April morning, I ignored the little man of good advice talking like a magpie in my head that said: *No, no, don't do it, don't jump. You have survived three jumps today. That should be enough for any dumb-ass half-breed.*

I did my usual dumb-ass, daredevil move anyway. Heck, there it was, twenty-five feet of open air with a nice, soft bed of sand in the landing zone. That is if you did the math right and didn't go four feet in any other direction. Then you would find the discarded concrete, rebar, and rubble. Let me tell you, brother, you don't want to know how that feels.

As my feet departed the safety of the overhang, I knew I was in deep dog crap. Oh, heck yeah, I had my main man, big Magoo, at the bottom of the sand pit. Magoo had made his third successful jump and was cheering me on. "Jump, you mother-fudged, half-breed punk," he screeched at the top of his lungs. Yes, we were trying to stop cussing. I thought, *Damn the pain! I've got to work on that cussing.* The people working at Tanks Football Stadium looked in our direction. They could hear every word his black ass was saying.

Magoo and I had run the streets of Ironton, Ohio for years. He was a black twelve-year-old and already six feet tall. I was a half-breed Indian the same age. Magoo always called me his half-breed midget brother. He was twelve inches taller than me; we were a perfect fit.

Magoo's given name was William. I am not sure who first nicknamed him "Wild Bill Magoo," or when, but he wouldn't answer to anything but Magoo now. I can guarantee you why they nicknamed him Magoo. His eyeglasses were as thick as Cold Wave cola bottles, and when he was without his glasses, he was as blind as the cartoon character Mr. Magoo.

We always did dumb-ass, dangerous stunts other than the sand pit jumping. We would explore the storm drain system and look for routes that went completely under the city leading to the Ohio River banks. We used only a half-burned-out light and a homemade spear to battle the river rats, and God only knows what other critters that were living in that darkness.

We once saw a critter coming towards us weighing about seventy-five pounds with one fire-red eyeball, fangs, and an odor as if it had already died. That fudge bar Magoo almost killed me coming out of that storm drain! I could almost stand up inside it. But Magoo, being six feet tall and having to duck walk, still plowed over me. He screamed like a little girl all the way, with a rooster tail of water flying behind him.

On numerous other outings, with other members of the gang of dumb-asses (as Grandma Lu appropriately named us), we would go to the hills north of Frog Town. Legend has it that Frog Town is the name the Indians used for Ironton, Ohio. As the legend goes, the flat river bottoms (where the town is now built) was a flood plain during the Indian times, with back-water bogs where hordes of frogs and catfish would get trapped. When the water receded, they could be caught by hand.

We would go to the Indian hills behind Ironton and find an old, sour grapevine, and would use it to swing over a gorge that had a fifty-foot drop into a dry creek bed. We had a rescue hook ready if a rider got stranded somewhere in between. That worked well for excitement until one of the gang slipped off and fractured his arm. Then it only took a few minutes for his older brother to climb that buckeye tree and cut out the Tarzan swing we had made.

We also had the brilliant idea to swim on the outlet side of the Greenup Locks and Dam. You can't imagine the undertow and the crazy currents. Grandma Lu told us, "You dumb-asses keep playing with fire, you will burn your asses, and then you will have to sit on the sore." *Oh, of course, I had to* make that old Indian witch a prophet. *Now I am going to catch three kinds of hell.* No, I was not allowed to be in that sand pit on this or any other day.

On top of all that, I was supposed to be helping Grandmas Lu and Wick hunt for the weeds and herbs they needed to brew their Shawnee spring elixir. They made the concoction so they could clean out their bowels of all the winter's poisons. If you want something dangerous, go to their house when they finish taking the spring elixir; the shit starts to flow! God help you, now that's living on the edge!

All of those thoughts spun in my head as I went in and out of sanity from the blinding pain from my fall. No, to be more accurate, the pain was from the sudden stop on top of that concrete rubble. Now I wished I had been in the woods looking for the weeds and stuff to make that elixir. Heck, I would have traded this mess of pain for a sniff of that elixir blown out from my two old grandmas' behinds!

OK, my road dog Magoo did not abandon me, but the blurred look on his face tells me I must be DOG (that is, dead on the ground). Oh, no, he just tried to move me, and I felt something in my nut sack rip. "Stop!" I screamed. As I motioned Magoo to come closer, I asked him to either go for help or let me die. "Hey! Magoo, you butt-wipe, I just did a damn header in this God-forsaken sand pit. Do you think you could go for some help?" You would believe that a person with one toe in the grave would not use this much bad language, but hell no! I needed some damn help!

I bet you would have guessed by now that this was not my first rodeo at getting myself messed up. This past winter my brothers, Bub and Mike, and I were bumper hopping after a heavy snowfall. All was going well. We would run out from our hiding place at a stop sign and grab onto a car's bumper. The car would slowly pull out, and we'd get a nice, slow ride to the next street. The slow, simple slide on our shoe leather didn't quite work out the way we had planned.

You would think that having lived thirteen years on this earth would have smartened me up a little more to danger. Oh, heck no! I was as dumb in the head as a hog was in the ass. You guessed it, my Grandma Lu said that. Yep, she was full of witty sayings.

The ride started out good, then things began to go very bad. Nothing on this ride went according to the Olympic manual for car bumper hopping. The speed was the first thing we noticed. This guy was floor boarding the dang car. The snow coming from the rear tires would smack us in our faces, and the driver swerved from one curb to another. OK, at this point in our ride, Bub and Wiggy (that was our nickname for Mike) bailed out. But no, not me. I was going to get my money's worth.

What happened next is the way legends get started. I hung in there. I gripped that bumper for all I was worth. For a short distance, I lost my footing and went to sliding on my knees. But at this point, the car was going too fast to bail safely. *Oh, look at me, thinking about safety while hanging onto the end of a car bumper doing about thirty-five miles per hour!* The only other thing I was concerned about was ruining my only pair of school shoes. Should have thought that one out a little more before grabbing onto the back end of a runaway car.

I got back on my feet. Just ahead, I could see a stop sign. The driver was not slowing down to allow me an easy exit. In fact, he blew right through the stop sign. *Maybe I could put him under citizen's arrest for blowing a stop sign.* I only had a second to ponder this.

As I looked to my left, I could see we were going to be T-boned by a car coming down the other street. Then it became perfectly clear; I needed to bail off this roller coaster ride! I angled towards the right curb as my driver tried to avoid the collision. I hit the curb at a break-neck speed, landing in a very soft snow bank. Only later would I learn that I had no broken bones.

No one in either vehicle was seriously hurt, but my driver was taken to jail for DUI. The police were happy that the poor Johnson kid that was crossing the street minding his own business was not killed. I guess they didn't see my shoe leather smoking and believed that the drunk's story about gremlins trying to crawl over his car trunk was the insane ranting of a drunk having delirious thoughts.

Meanwhile, back in the sand pit, through my glaze of pain, I saw my rescuers on the path leading to the landing zone. I could now see my cousin Big Slim (no problem identifying him from a distance because he was six-foot-eight-inches tall), and my older brother Bub. *Good going, Magoo. You brought some muscle to get my dumb-ass out of here.*

Bub had tried to warn me of the dangers of the pit. He told me the sand pit girls would someday trap me down there and give me the wax job of my life. Oh yeah, my curiosity got the best of me, and I had to ask what a wax job was! He looked at me with his most serious expression and said, "You're not old enough to know, but keep coming here and you will find out first hand."

As I drifted in and out of delirium, I thought that I could see the pit girls coming towards me with a giant mallet. My vision focused on a figure at the rim of the pit looking at the mess I had made of myself. It was Grandma Lu and was she going to be ticked! She was most likely hoping I was dead.

Only two days before this tragic sporting event, she tried to kill me. That's right, justifiable homicide as I recall. I had been working like a borrowed bank mule cutting kindling wood and mowing the weeds of a lawn for her, only expecting a small slice of fry bread with butter and homemade blackberry jam. Oh, but no! She told me to come by a little later. I couldn't accept that. My only thought was to use my daddy's loving nickname for my Grandma Lu.

That's right, I called her a crazy, old Indian witch. In my haste to make a new opening in her screen door, it may have sounded like "bitch" instead of "witch." I hit the back porch on the fly. With one mighty leap, I cleared to the middle of her backyard. No way would she catch me!

My only mistake was not grabbing the kindling hatchet next to the door. But Grandma Lu sure didn't miss it! I could hear that tomahawk come whooshing through the air. All I could think was, *Feet don't fail me now!* The woodcutting hatchet hit the heel of my shoe and ricocheted between my legs. I just knew she was aiming for my crotch.

Indians have this uncanny ability to cripple their prey and move in for a slow kill by taking the scalp next, and then the remaining body parts. I made the turn in the gravel-covered alley at about thirty miles per hour, throwing a rooster tail of slag into the air as I headed for the sanctuary of my main man Magoo's house.

After I had felt there was enough distance between myself and that crazy, old Indian witch, I stopped to take inventory of my body parts. Yes, my boys were still hanging in there! My Converse heel would need a little patch work. But, all in all, I was in good shape, thanks in part to my tremendous speed, and my Grandma Lu not practicing enough with her tomahawk.

Back to the sand pit incident. The rescue team was surrounding me. As they were lifting me out of the sand, I was fading in and out of reality. I thought I saw the rear of my beloved Tanks Football Stadium behind Ironton High School. My vision was fading in and out.

The next place I saw was the back door of Grandma Lu's house. I heard someone saying "Cuttaywah matchamanetto" to Magoo, which meant "black devil get your ass moving down the road before I put a boot in it." I was relatively sure that could only be one person, Grandma Lu.

Magoo knew she was serious. I sure hated that poor Magoo was getting the blame for my stupidity. But it sure wasn't the first time, and most likely not the last.

I wish there were a way to erase memories, even when the memories are from the fog of an Indian drug-induced coma. Yes, the old grandmas were working their Indian magic, or witchcraft, or whatever you call it. I had poultices on parts of my body that you don't want to know how they got there. For sure the grandmas had an opportunity to see me naked. Now that should not be a bad thing, knowing they were trying to help.

Maybe they were saving my life from my old daddy. He always promised the Johnson tribe that if any of us cost him money by getting injured (because he had no medical coverage) or cost him money concerning other people's property, we should hope to be DOA. Because if we were not dead, he would take us out himself. Trust me, I did not doubt his veracity and willingness to follow up on this promise. So, my grandmas were saving my life once again. If they got a look at my crusty behind, no big deal.

The days turned into a week, and I could start to move a little with the help of my beloved grandmas. My old Grandma Wick was not much help. But at ninety-two years old she could surprise you at times.

Bub liked to harass Grandma Wick. He would always laugh about her grabbing him around his throat with her boney hands and telling him that she would choke the life out of his hellgrammite-ass. One time she put pressure around his pencil neck and as he started turning purple, I thought he was going to pass out. But she slacked up, and he peed his pants instead. That time Grandma Wick got the last laugh.

I came out of a deep sleep to the pungent aroma of Grandma Wick's kinnikinnick-filled, stone, Indian pipe. Herbs, tobacco, tree barks, and God only knows what other crap was in that mix. All I know is that you could get a real buzz just by being in the same room when she fired up a bowlful.

Another aroma was coming from Grandma Lu's kitchen. Yum! She had fresh bread baking in the oven and a big Slye chicken frying on the cooktop. The greatest family pride (to this date) was explained to me by Grandma Wick this past year when I asked, "What *is* a Slye chicken?" She looked at me with a foxy grin, then revealed a great story.

During the flu pandemic of 1918-1919, she and my Grandma Lu were using their Indian medicines to save as many lives as they could. Grandma Lu just had her nineteenth birthday when they traveled by horse and wagon to Duck Run Road in Scioto County, Ohio to help the Slye family. They worked their magic and were especially proud of saving seven-year-old Leonard Franklin Slye. Now I was not too impressed with that name until they told me that Leonard grew up to become "King of the Cowboys" Roy Rogers. Now *that* was impressive!

The pay from the Slye family for their Indian medicine magic was two fat hens. Roy's father, Andrew, told my grandmas to keep those chickens in the bag until they got back to Lawrence County. Then ring the necks, gut and pluck them birds, drop them in the fat, and fry them as quick as possible. If the High Sheriff came around, do not tell him they were Scioto County yard birds.

At first, I thought Grandma Wick had fallen asleep with the stone, Indian pipe between her teeth, dangling as if it was going to fall to the floor. Then, her eyes popped open, and she started speaking in broken Shawnee. Now I don't speak Shawnee, but I am sure it was not German. She then started telling me the most mind-blowing story I had ever heard!

In the past, she had told short tales of our Indian heritage, and stories like the Slye chicken incident, which made my chest pump up with pride. But ***this*** story came as a coherent chronicled map of our family's troubled journey from Prophetstown on the Tippecanoe River to southern Ohio, and our relationship to the great Shawnee Chief Tecumseh.

CHAPTER 2

Prophetstown   November 1811   on the Tippecanoe

Ciicothe's spirits had taken a nose dive on this cold, dank day. The clouds had gotten heavy with moisture that felt as if it was ice. Due to the early November cold, this drizzle could change to snow at any time. The people had the blessings of the Great Good Spirit to have had five days of warm, pleasant weather. That allowed for the gathering of the much needed native herbs, roots, tree barks, buckeyes, and other vital plants to supply the medicines for the people's health through the looming, winter, hunger moon.

Ciicothe, at twelve summers old, was working as a gatherer of the ancient medicine plants. Great responsibilities were on her young shoulders. Her aunt, Tall Walker Woman (who was her adoptive (Nekkaem) mother), was also her teacher in the medicine craft. Tall Walker Woman (Quinoxetheitock Ochqwe) and her Uncle Yellow Robe (Neseethe) had adopted Ciicothe along with her older brother Little Hawk (Matsquathay Peleethay). With the untimely death of their mother and father, they were made orphans at a young age. All they had known in their short lives was pain.

Ciicothe's father died in a battle with the long knives on the Maumee River three months before her birth. She was birthed on the banks of that same long knives blood-filled river. Her father and Uncle Yellow Robe were Delaware Indians from the Ohio Tuscarawas River country. The two young brothers had escaped the March 1782 massacre of the Christian Delaware Indians at the Moravian mission town of Gnadenhutten on the Tuscarawas River.

Uncle Yellow Robe was cudgeled, scalped and had his manhood mutilated, yet survived. The brothers were tough Delaware Indians, but the Shawnee people had accepted them as their own. Uncle Yellow Robe continued his pacifist Christian ways, working as a medicine man for the health of the Shawnee people. Ciicothe's father turned to the Kispokothe Sept and the war path. The remainder of the Christian Delaware Indians at "huts of grace" were massacred by militiamen from Pennsylvania.

The Delaware Indian people had returned to this place only wanting to harvest crops to ward off starvation during the remainder of the winter. Their reward was the murder of twenty-eight men, twenty-nine women, and thirty-nine children. Her father and Uncle Yellow Robe were the only survivors to tell the sad, Christian story of this massacre.

Ciicothe's mother was part of the Maykujay Sept, and also a member of Tecumseh's family. She took care of the health, medicines and food gathering for the support of the South Wind people. Ciicothe's mother died six years after Ciicothe's birth in Ohio's Prophetstown by contracting the white man's smallpox from the inoculation she was given. The evil medicine provided by the long knives was intended to help the people and prevent this dreaded white man's scourge. Instead, it killed her mother as if they had thrust the long knife into her heart. Many of the Shawnee people died that summer moon of 1805 from the white devil's poison.

The cold drizzle change to the weather (Matcheykeesek) was not the only reason for Ciicothe's and the Shawnee people's sinking hearts. For many days the news of the approach of a massive long knife army, commanded by the white devil (Wahcanaquah Cuttaywah), the evil General Harrison, was on the war path heading in their direction.

The people's weakened state was a great danger for them. The hunters were gone trying to fill the meat needs for the people, which would help them survive the coming cold, hunger moon of the fast approaching winter. Ciicothe's brother, Little Hawk, was on his first hunt (a time of great pride for him), and had not returned. Tecumseh's braves were on a mission to the north. The protection of Prophetstown would now fall to the old, the sick, the women, and the few hunters that had returned early. All this was under the leadership of the one-eyed prophet, Tenskwatawa, who Ciicothe believed had lost his mind.

Ciicothe had watched the prophet with growing fear of his erratic behavior. He would walk from one end of Prophetstown to the other, all the while talking to their dead ancestors. Sometimes he stopped and turned his head to the sky with the cold rain pelting his face, and scream at the top of his range, which was breaking what little confidence Ciicothe had in his leadership.

Ciicothe was ripped out of her daydreaming by the all too familiar screaming voice of Tall Walker Woman. "Ciicothe! What are you doing? The work will not get done by walking around with your head in your ass. Go to our wigwam and stay out of the concerns of the old prophet. All the medicine roots and buckeyes need proper storage. Go now!" This exchange needed no response from Ciicothe. When Tall Walker Woman spoke in that tone, Ciicothe knew she intended business.

She ran at breakneck speed all the way to their wigwam, only chancing a short glance in Tall Walker Woman's direction, who was leaning on her makeshift cane near the chief's council house. All of the excitement of the one-eyed prophet's activities, along with his gray-haired council, only elevated Ciicothe's already high anxiety.

After entering their wigwam, Ciicothe began busying herself by lining the deep holes with dry straw for the hole-up storage of the supply of medicine roots, all the while knowing Tall Walker Woman was hobbling in her direction on her broken foot and leg. Ciicothe knew without a doubt that Tall Walker Woman would plant her good foot into her ass if she weren't doing her tasks.

Two days earlier Tall Walker Woman had fallen down a steep, dry-cut ravine breaking her leg, foot, and wrist. This would be bad for a young person, but for an old person, it could be life ending. With all the added stress and terror of the approach of a massive long knife army, her mother had good reason to be on edge.

Tall Walker Woman entered the wigwam crying, trying her best to hide her face. Ciicothe asked, "Mother, what is the matter?" Her hesitation to answer made the hair stand up on Ciicothe's neck, her worst fear was an evacuation of Prophetstown. Due to Tall Walker Woman's broken condition, she would not be permitted to go. She would slow the people down when they needed a rapid retreat. Numerous sick and old could not go, leaving their lives and fate to the mercy of the long knives' evil war chief, General Harrison.

Through her sobs, Tall Walker Woman instructed Ciicothe how to pack the vital herbs along with the prepared medicines for a run to the north with the tribe. Ciicothe protested, insisting she was going to stay with her mother. Tall Walker Woman wouldn't have it, nor would she listen to Ciicothe's argument. Tall Walker Woman insisted that she would be safe. Ciicothe could see the fear in her mother's eyes, and began to sob as she started to do what Tall Walker Woman had instructed. Ciicothe could only think that this was the end of life as she had known it.

The morning came with a clap of thunder in the snow-filled sky, which was a bad omen. Horror and screams filled the darkness that was still hiding the sun. The South Wind people were running in panic. Their family members, who had been standing watch over the long knives' massive encampment, were returning to Prophetstown, wounded and carried by others. They were either dead or near death. The acrid smoke filled the air, an occasional ring of a musket could be heard in the distance along with the screams of the injured. The panic to evacuate Prophetstown had begun.

Uncle Yellow Robe entered the wigwam. He was all business while asking Ciicothe for the medicine hide-bags. He was looking at his beloved Tall Walker Woman the entire time he was talking with Ciicothe. Ciicothe knew there could be no crying, all the tears would be in their hearts.

Old Uncle Yellow Robe bowed his head to pray an English, Christian prayer, which Ciicothe knew most of the words. She wished that the long knife, General Harrison, and his army would live by the sacred Bible words that her beloved Uncle Yellow Robe and Tall Walker Woman had always lived by in their hearts. They always believed in the teachings of the man Jesus.

Uncle Yellow Robe went out of the wigwam quickly. Without words, he indicated for Ciicothe to follow with her supply of medicine roots and prepared medicines. Ciicothe obeyed her uncle's wishes. The pain to leave her beloved mother behind was eating a hole in her heart.

Ciicothe and the South Wind people were on the muddy trail moving north of town as fast as the vast throng of people escaping certain death could move. The pain of leaving your home and some of your family behind was new for Ciicothe. She could see in the faces of the old people the countless scars of this type of horror carved in their spirits.

The crying of the small children healthy enough to make this escape was drowned out by the screams of the sick children and the old that were left behind in Prophetstown. This echoed in her heart as well as a vision of Tall Walker Woman being murdered in their wigwam. Ciicothe knew in her heart what she needed to do. She asked the two young boys that were helping carry the bundles of medicines and herbs to take what she was carrying. Relieved of her burden, she ran for the town in the hope of saving her mother.

Ciicothe arrived in Prophetstown to screams of agony. Using as much caution as time would permit, she circled toward the back of the line of wigwams next to the chief's large council house. She was hoping to enter the rear of their wigwam through her secret opening. This opening had saved her behind from a whipping more times than she could count! The opening was near the root storage pits dug on the outer perimeter of their wigwam. Providing she had not filled the center pit with root storage, she could crawl underground a short distance into this empty space.

Ciicothe's heart was beating out of her chest as she arrived at the rear of the wigwam. She felt the long knives would hear her heart beating, kill her, and ruin her chance to save her beloved mother. As she made her way through the opening, moving like a groundhog, she was quickly in the root storage pit. There was plenty of space for her, but for Tall Walker Woman she would need to dig the tunnel bigger to quicken their escape into the ravine at the rear of the town.

Ciicothe slowly lifted the cover only to have her heart sink in despair. Two of the evil Harrison's long knives were already in the wigwam. One was standing over Tall Walker Woman with her hair gripped in one hand and a knife at her neck. Ciicothe felt hopeless. She saw the tomahawk leaning on the wall next to the fourth pit from her, but was unsure of what she could do with it, or if she could even reach it. She had to try something.

Ciicothe made her move as the first long knife departed their wigwam with his arms loaded with stolen property. The long knife that was holding Tall Walker Woman screamed some profanity at her mother as she tried to wrench away. She bit off the fingers of the hand that had been holding her hair. He instantly reacted by cutting her throat from ear to ear, almost severing her head from her body.

Ciicothe was blinded with tears; a silent scream welled in her chest. In unbridled anger, she burst out of the pit and grabbed the tomahawk. Before the evil long knife could react, she split his skull between his eyes, sending his brains flying into the hot, open, fire pit. The mess started to sizzle before his twitching body hit the bare, earthen floor. Ciicothe had never hit anything that hard. She continued to smash the tomahawk into his mangled head then turned her attention to her mother. There was no hope, she was gone.

Ciicothe looked at the long knife's fingers protruding from Tall Walker Woman's mouth. *If there is any justice, maybe this is it.* She gently took the fingers out of her mother's mouth and tossed them into the fire pit. She removed the hand-carved cross and placed it around her own neck, the blood of her beloved mother was still dripping from the body of the man Jesus carved on the front of the cross.

Ciicothe knew her time was drawing short. She had to try to make the run back north to catch up with her people, or all would be lost. She gathered two more totes filled with food and medicines and loaded them into the root pit. Then she returned to say one more prayer at the side of her fallen mother.

As Ciicothe finished the Shawnee prayer for her mother's afterlife on the Great Good Spirit's mystic river town, the other long knife returned with a burning torch in his hand. As he was surveying the mess, he saw Ciicothe with the tomahawk in her hand, and the blood and brains mixture all over her face. He must have realized it was too late to save his friend, and backed out of the wigwam with shock and fear in his eyes.

Ciicothe could hear the screams of the old and the sick being burned alive throughout the town. Having seen the tomahawk in Ciicothe's hand, and not wanting to fight her in closed quarters, this coward of a soldier had decided fire was the fate that would be her end. Starting at the entrance door, he set flames that quickly grew.

Wanting to leave, Ciicothe moved towards the root storage pit where her secret exit was hidden. But the long knife was now at the rear of the wigwam setting more of it on fire. She could hear his panting breath hissing foul, English cuss words damning her to hell. She didn't have much time for idle thoughts. However: *If anyone has a free ride into white man's hell, it is surely these evil long knives and their leaders.*

Ciicothe made it into the root pit and turned to exit the secret tunnel, but she got stuck with the two totes full of the needed supplies. She knew that if she were to survive the journey north to reunite with her beloved South Wind people, she would need this food and medicine. Ciicothe pushed through the tunnel holding the first tote bag in front of her face, praying the long knife had returned to his work of stealing their town's property. She was in luck, he was nowhere in sight.

She placed the first tote into the woods heading into the steep ravine where her mother had fallen. She ran back into the opening, sliding on her belly like an otter. She could now feel the heat from the fire in the root storage pit. She could smell the roots in the other storage pits cooking, and the pungent smell of human flesh burning throughout the town, all the while knowing that some of that flesh was her mother. Ciicothe knew she had to hurry, her clothing was now starting to smoke. The heat was getting unbearable. She was now smelling her own flesh burn.

Ciicothe was in the tunnel with the second tote, tomahawk, and knife used to cut her mother's throat; she was pushing all of this in front of her face while exiting the tunnel. As she reached the opening, she could see the long knife had returned and set fire to the wigwam next in line. More screams were coming from inside. With every scream, a huge smile would cross this dog's face. She could see that he loved his evil work.

Ciicothe had to make a run for the woods or she would burn to death in her family's wigwam. She saw her chance. Gathering her necessary things, she darted towards the woods. She had made it but realized that her hair and clothing on the right side of her body was on fire. She knew that she couldn't stop, so she scooped up the other tote on a dead run.

At breakneck speed, she made it to the bottom of the ravine to the God-sent water of a small creek in which she extinguished the fire. She knew she had been burned. The pain on her face and arm was excruciating. She looked back at the town, homes, and food supply, all had been either burned or pillaged. Her heart burst with more pain than she could hold, and she passed out.

Ciicothe awoke to cold water running onto her face. The small creek was now growing as the rain, mixed with sleet and snow, was adding to its flow. The sun had traveled to its night home, the cold was now creeping into her bones. Ciicothe knew she must get to some type of shelter so that what remained of her burned clothing could dry. The hide totes were high on the bank, safe from washing away. Her only chance for survival was inside them.

Ciicothe moved with the speed of Mother Turtle. Her bones ached from the cold. The burns on her face and arm were now growing numb. She remembered there was a hunters' cave close in the southwest direction from Prophetstown. She knew that she must get there before all the firewood became too wet to start a lifesaving fire. Ciicothe thought that her need for the warmth of a fire now, compared to her escape through fire, was somewhat funny. Yet the pain of her face and arm reminded her that none of this evil day was a laughing matter.

Ciicothe easily found the hidden hunters' cave. She was hoping to find a supply of wood and flint to help her start a fire. There was no flint and only a small amount of kindling with the firewood supply. She would have to go back out into the cold, raw night. The thought of this made her collapse to the cave floor and sob uncontrollably. As she was shivering with a fever that was now consuming her life, she passed out into a dream state.

Ciicothe dreamt of the pleasant sounds of the joyous South Wind people at the ceremony of the green corn moon. The faithful people were giving thanks, not only for the harvest of the corn but also for the abundance of squash, beans, pumpkins, sunflowers, sweet potatoes and tobacco. Ciicothe snapped out of this dream into the nightmare that was now her reality, and the cold that now penetrated her soul and spirit. She was not sure how long she had slept.

Ciicothe remembered the smell of firewood burning as she made her way to this hunters' cave. Maybe she could find this camp's fire unattended and steal some hot coals to start her cave fire. But first, she needed a supply of dry firewood. It was easily found. Next to the cave was some deadfall protected by a rock overhang that kept it dry. With the help of the blood and brains crusted tomahawk, this find provided several loads of wood.

Ciicothe was searching the woods trying to locate the campfire with only her sense of smell. It was now totally dark and the rain was replaced by snow coming from the driving, bitter, north wind. Ciicothe could not believe her eyes! As she cleared the crest of a small hill, she saw a fire in the distance. Mayhap her luck had changed, and the goodness of the Great Good Spirit would guide her to the source of this lifesaving fire.

Ciicothe circled the camp with as much stealth that her weakened condition would allow. As she became aware that it was not occupied, she realized that this was not a campfire, but a grave fire set on top of the buried dead to help mask their odor. This was a long knives trick to save the bodies from being consumed by wolves, birds of prey, and other animals who scavenge the land.

Knowing this site was not occupied, Ciicothe would be free to collect the fire she needed. She found some of white man's cloth to make a torch, ensuring she could return to the hunters' cave with a start of the life-giving fire. She would then be able to eat and prepare the medicines needed to treat her burns.

Ciicothe made her torch and dabbed the cloth into some pine sap. After lighting the torch, she turned to go, and a bitter cold ripped through her body. She started up the hill that led back to the cave. She was sure she had heard the moan of a man from the grave, which made her waste the last of her energy by running the entire distance to the protection of the hunters' cave.

Ciicothe awoke to the sound of the wind howling outside the warmth of the cave. She ate and then made the medicines. They were already having a positive effect on her fever and burns. She could still hear the sounds of the moans coming from the burning grave in her mind. The thought of someone being buried alive was too much for her to take, even if it was a white man. She could not be sure, or sane, without returning to the gravesite.

With her buckskin dress in tatters from the fire, Ciicothe realized she needed clothes. There was a chance that a dead soldier could provide her with them. Needing comfort and peace of mind that some poor soul was not alive in his own grave, she knew what she must do.

Ciicothe arrived at the gravesite but wished to be in the warm cave next to the cozy fire pit. She set to the work of unearthing the bodies. She moved some of the smoldering wood. As she started to remove the thin layer of soil, she located the body of a lifeless soldier. Using the tomahawk as a tool, she continued to dig. As the head was exposed, she saw that this man had been shot between the eyes. The sight of this somehow made her retch and fall backwards.

This man had been scalped, which gave the idea that her people were the cause of these deaths. Ciicothe fell to her knees, giving a prayer in both Shawnee and English. Her heart was not in robbing this grave, although the white man had robbed her ancestors' graves and burial mounds since their arrival more than two hundred years ago.

Ciicothe returned to her work of removing the soldier's shirt and britches. The clothing was too large for her, but she would find a way to use them. The next soldier's grave proved to be a man closer to her size. As she was taller than the average twelve-year-old Shawnee girl, his clothing should fit, serving her needs. This man had suffered the same fate as the first.

When Ciicothe moved to the third gravesite (what she thought would be the last), she distinctly heard a moan from the grave. She fell back, not trusting her ears. To her shock, she saw a hand scratching through the thin layer of soil and smoldering wood.

Ciicothe sprang into action pulling the smoldering wood off the grave, then cautiously started digging. Relieved of the weight of the wood, the long knife soldier raised to a sitting position. He gasped for air, and spit dirt and blood from his mouth. Ciicothe fell backwards from the horror of this sight. It reminded her of one of Uncle Yellow Robe's Bible stories, making her lose her water.

The man started to plead in a dry, cracked voice, "Help Me! Help Me!" With some compassion in her heart for this tragic site, Ciicothe got to her feet. Considering the events of the past two days, it would take all of her strength not to use the tomahawk on this half-dead man by cracking his skull open, and moving on to find her people. As she moved closer, she could see this man had also been shot in the head.

The blood running into his mouth from his scalp wound had dried, giving him a mask of terror. He choked several times saying, "Water, please, water!" Ciicothe got a handful of wet snow. It gave this broken man the much-needed moisture to clear his airway and mouth of Mother Earth, who had come close to taking his spirit back to her bosom. Ciicothe knew that this white man would be in some way vital to her life. The Great Good Spirit would show the path when the time was right.

CHAPTER 3

Terre Haute   1811-1813   on the Wabash

Ciicothe woke early while the white man, who called himself Hiram the Masonic, lay sleeping peacefully for the first time in three days. She learned that his name was Hiram David of Harrodsburg, Kentucky. With much effort, Ciicothe had assisted Hiram on the return to the hunters' cave. As she cleaned his wounds, she realized the one on his head had not penetrated his skull.

Hiram also had a shoulder injury that she treated with her medicines. She dressed the wounds with a bandage made from the top shirt of his dead Masonic Brothers. This man was blessed by the Great Good Spirit. The only serious injury he had was the new part in his hair where the round bounced off his hard skull, only to remove the scalp from his head.

Ciicothe prepared the last of the food that she had taken from the now ruined Prophetstown. They would have to move on or starve in this place. There was no use returning to Prophetstown, as everything there had been looted or burned.

Hiram woke with a start. He raised up with a guttural scream from within his soul as if he had entered the long knife's hell, or had he dreamed he was still buried in the ground? Hiram looked at Ciicothe, calmed himself, and then started to talk in a nervous voice harsh to her ear. As in the past three days, he talked incessantly. At times Ciicothe wished the blood-soaked mud was still clogging his mouth, then she would be free of his noise. Some of his words were new to her. She tried to understand, but fell short of his intended meaning.

As Ciicothe listened, she learned that the Shawnee people did not kill his Masonic Brothers, nor bury him alive. She was not surprised. The evil work was that of Harrison's thugs following their evil leader's orders to silence their voices forever, making it look as if the Shawnee braves had done this deed. The Masonic Brothers had uncovered the real reason for this massive force. It was not to parley in a position of strength with the Shawnee leaders as they were first told. But a force to massacre the entire tribe leaving no survivors to tell the story. As Hiram said, "On the square and level."

The Masonic Brothers decided to return to Kentucky wanting no part of this blood bath, but this was not to be. Harrison's thugs followed them to the location where Ciicothe had found them. They had disarmed and killed his Brothers and thought they had done the same to him. However, they had only knocked him stupid, incapacitating him so as to permit his burial. His resurrection was assisted by his newfound angel. Hiram fully believed that God had sent Ciicothe and the cold rain to save his life for some greater purpose. He thanked God for this.

As Hiram finished his story, Ciicothe's head was spinning. She felt she had understood the long knives' greed before (with their passions for the theft of other's property) but now was really unsure. She felt as if she could never trust white man, a tribe of people that would kill their own out of greed. Mayhap she had a good feeling for this white man. Mayhap she had no choice to feel this way, as she needed his help to return to her people. Ciicothe would keep her tomahawk close at hand.

Ciicothe and Hiram departed the safety of the hunters' cave. Following the flow of the Wabash River, they walked cautiously towards the southwest for two days. Unwilling to start a fire, starvation began to show in their faces, and their bones ached from the cold. The nutrition of the small amount of forage they had gathered was gone.

Hiram had developed a plan to get help from his Masonic Brother who lived on the Wabash, the place the French men called the high earth, Terre Haute. He could provide them safety from Harrison's goons, as well as food and a place to heal before the journey to reunite with their families. She understood most of what Hiram had said, but her trust of any white man was weak.

Ciicothe had Uncle Yellow Robe's tomahawk close at hand, and she would split Hiram's skull if he crossed her. As they walked, she held the wooden cross with the man Jesus carved on it in one hand, and the bloody, brain-crusted tomahawk in the other. She found that these possessions gave her some measure of comfort and strength to go on.

With Hiram leading the way, they topped a high hill overlooking a beautiful section of the Wabash River Valley. In the distance, on a high bluff overlooking the river, smoke was curling from the chimney of a cabin made from logs. The tall trees along this run of the river were cleared, which created good farm land. The stubble of corn stalks and other harvested crops stood through the dusting of fresh snow.

The scene reminded Ciicothe of the farm fields around Prophetstown. There were wigwams, the long council house, and the happy South Wind people working to provide the needs of life. A tear fell from her eye and rolled down the scarred tissue of her face.

They approached the cabin from the wooded area's protection with caution, as Harrison's men occupied a fort close to this location. Ciicothe and Hiram believed they were marked for dead if found. The cabin had no windows, only thick, wood shutters with gun ports at the openings where windows should be located. The only entrance door was of thick, oak wood reinforced with cross beams of solid oak timbers. The house was built for safety on this dangerous frontier.

As Ciicothe and Hiram approached the cabin, a long, gun barrel penetrated the gun port to the right of the door. With a booming, French-accented voice, a man said, "Don't come one step closer."

Ciicothe gripped the blood-stained tomahawk tighter. *This must be a comical sight to the persons in the cabin, a half-burned Indian girl ready to fight.*

The man called out again, asking, "Hoosier?"

"It is I, Hiram, seeking a length of cable tow with the help from my trusted Brother," Hiram replied.

The door burst open! Out ran a tall, thin man with the most beautiful headdress she had ever seen on any chief or warrior during her short life! He also had a long, flowing mustache that grew to the bottom of his chin. She moved slowly forward while Hiram ran to greet his Masonic Brother with a bear hug. A joyous conversation followed, which seemed to go on for hours.

Ciicothe was surprised to see a beautiful Indian woman walk through the heavy door, leading a small boy by the hand, coming towards them with hesitation and caution. There was little wonder at her slow approach. This beautiful woman must have thought that Ciicothe looked hideous with her half-burned face, hair, and arm. Being dressed in the clothing of a poor militiaman, and covered with dirt and dried blood, she most likely couldn't tell that Ciicothe was a girl, mayhap not even human.

They entered the cabin with all the fuss as if Ciicothe and Hiram were long lost family. But Ciicothe remained tense, gripping her tomahawk. After the introductions, food preparation was their first priority for they had not eaten in two days. The food and drink were the best Ciicothe had ever tasted. It was better than any meal prepared during the hunger moon or green corn ceremonies.

Through her weak command of English, Ciicothe learned that the Indian woman was French's wife, Morning Star, a Potawatomi from the north. The young boy was little Pete, their only son. He was just two years old. Ciicothe understood that French was a trapper, as was his father and grandfather. His mother was a full-blooded Kickapoo of the Kankakee River Tribe, leaving French to be called a half-breed by the long knife whites. He often used his skill as a translator.

Ciicothe continued to listen but was lost in the conversation. She wished she had learned more English from her beloved Tall Walker Woman or Uncle Yellow Robe when they read the white man's good book to her. The conversation drifted between English, French, and some type of Masonic tongue, which lost her completely. She could only use sign language to successfully communicate with Morning Star.

The weeks went by quickly. Both Ciicothe and Hiram continued to heal from their separate hells, mentally and physically. Ciicothe cried much in her heart during the nights, but stayed busy during the day. She helped process the animal hides, a task Ciicothe was familiar with by having worked all her life at assigned tasks for support of the South Wind people. That effort helped her forget the pain of not knowing their fate.

December was full of joy with the marking of the man Jesus' birthday. There was much celebration, food, and gifts. Ciicothe was told that Jesus was now more than 1,800 summers old and that he had risen from the grave. She could not grasp this thought. *He must be in the land ruled by the hand of the Great Good Spirit, next to the River of Life.* Although Uncle Yellow Robe embraced the pacifist Christian path, he did not go to this extent of the Christmas ceremony. He only passed it with days of prayer and fasting.

As the spring season turned into summer, the time to finish planting the summer garden came. Ciicothe's spirits were as high as they had ever been since running from Prophetstown during the massacre of the South Wind people.

Choosing not to return to his family in Kentucky as planned, Hiram David had departed for the south in June. Fearing death at the hands of Harrison's thugs, he was going to start a new life and remain dead to them. He felt this was vital for his survival and that of his family.

Ciicothe's English had improved enough to understand Hiram's tearful good-bye and his promise to pay the debt of his saved life to her and her people. She knew this was coming from his heart. He then removed a beautiful emblem of the Masonic brotherhood from around his neck. He placed it over Ciicothe's head, giving her a gentle kiss. She would prize this gift for the remainder of her life.

Ciicothe had lived two summers with French, Morning Star, and little Pete. Her love for this family rivaled the love for her own family, and that of her beloved South Wind people. Ciicothe had mastered the use of English by improving her ability to read, write, and communicate the language.

The burn scars on the right side of Ciicothe's face, arm, and body had softened with time. The use of the ancient poultice (used for burns) that she learned to make from her Tall Walker Woman mother had worked miracles, but the scars on her heart would never heal. The South Wind people had no word for revenge, yet somehow Ciicothe understood this concept. If ever given the chance, she would take her just reward.

Ciicothe was working the harvest from their small, farm fields, trying to get as many of the late plants into storage before the onset of another winter season. Her thoughts drifted to finding a way to rejoin what might remain of her family or the South Wind Tribe. The war with the British redcoats had raged for over a year. As always, the Indians were pulled into the conflict.

French was forced to join Harrison's army as a translator. He served with distinction on two fronts, yet this was not enough for them. Three of Harrison's army thugs had returned on this September morning of 1813 to persuade French to go into the north country to use his translating skills. They tried to convince him that it was in great need for God and country. The real reason for this was their insatiable hunger for the lands of other people, to kill others (not like them), and take everything.

The meeting did not go well. Because French did not respect these people, he did not invite the soldiers into the cabin. They began shouting louder and louder. The tone was laced with more anger, and Harrison's thugs started spitting out white man's filthy words.

Ciicothe continued to gather the largest and healthiest seed for starting next year's garden. This effort was vital to the existence of this little family. She now had a full bag of dried bean seeds. Trying to ignore the heated discussion, she returned to the cabin to store this sacred stock. She heard gunfire, and her heart began to race. As she exited the cabin, she grabbed the old tomahawk.

The scene was chaotic. French was jerking around on the ground with a bloody hole in his forehead. Morning Star was kneeling beside him. Little Pete was being choked by a really mean-looking dog of a man who surely intended to kill him.

Ciicothe knew what she must do. She quickly drew the tomahawk back, ignoring the gun blast and the bullet speeding past her head. She leveled the blade of the hatchet on the left side of the thug's head. With a glancing blow, it took a large slice of his scalp and continued on to remove his left ear. The entire mess from his head hit the ground at the same time his body bounced off the rocky path.

Ciicothe turned to the other thug with a scream that would put fear in the devil himself. He was fumbling with his gun, which discharged harmlessly into the ground. Before Ciicothe could plant the tomahawk into this thug's forehead, the leader of the soldiers blindsided her, hitting her in the head with the butt of a long rifle. All her life lights went out. The only thing she could remember was a low-pitched, buzzing noise, like the arrival of the white man's flies.

CHAPTER 4

Vincennes   1813-1814   on the Wabash

Ciicothe could see the happy South Wind people dancing around the many open pit fires and the green corn decorating the wigwams throughout the beautiful Prophetstown. The Tippecanoe River was flowing clean and clear, fish were jumping, and the buffalo were seeking refuge from the late summer heat in the cool waters of this sacred river. She could hear the singing of a beautiful voice in a language unfamiliar to her.

The light was burning Ciicothe's right eye as she slowly regained consciousness. She cautiously opened her left eye to the sight of Morning Star and little Pete huddled together in the corner. This cabin was made of logs with three-inch air slots between each log. Firewood was stacked from floor to ceiling with only a small space for them to sit on dry corn shucks and kindling wood.

Morning Star was singing a Potawatomi funeral song, of which Ciicothe hoped was not for her. The mournful tone made Ciicothe wish she could return to the beautiful dream of Prophetstown and the happier times that did not include the long knives. Morning Star and little Pete saw Ciicothe waking from the coma she had been in for two days and rushed to her side. Ciicothe began to cry with them, she could feel the sting in her ruined right eye.

Ciicothe was sad having to relive the events that occurred in the dooryard at French's cabin. She received a mighty blow to her head, which smashed her right eye socket and part of her skull. It knocked her out cold for the trip to this prison located at the governor's Grouseland Estate.

French was dead. He was the victim of the angry master of arms who had gotten partial pay for his evil deed by having his ear removed by Ciicothe's tomahawk. The master of arms had survived. He told all that would listen to him the lie of a story about a giant, Indian warrior attacking him and smashing his skull, but he was able to put a slug in the big Indian's gut. He sure didn't want to tell the truth about how a ragged, half-burned, fourteen-year-old Indian girl lopped off part of his scalp with his entire ear attached.

The prisoners were locked in the wood storage cabin for two days with little food and water. They had only a slop jar for their sanitary relief, which was emptied only at the will of their captors. Morning Star's beautiful, handmade dress was stained with the blood of her beloved French. Ciicothe's torn and tattered dress was covered with blood from her now dead eye. Now she knew how the one-eyed prophet Tenskwatawa felt to have lived with one eye, only able to see half of the world.

The door for the wood storage cabin started to open, it was the soldier who had bashed in Ciicothe's head. He looked at her and said that he was pleased that she had lived. He laughed an evil laugh and said that old one-ear Moss would be very happy that she survived, so he could get his chance to stretch her neck with a hangman's rope. They only needed the final approval of Governor Harrison.

The soldier departed leaving a wooden tray of hog-slop table scraps and a wooden bucket of brackish Wabash River water with mud and leaves floating on the surface. They made the best of what was provided by straining the water through a cloth into a gourd dipper and making a meal out of the slop. Each prayed and gave thanks for the nourishment.

Ciicothe knew that without having her medicine bag, she would most surely lose the sight in her right eye or even die. She was told that French's cabin had been burned, and their property was taken by Harrison's thugs. Ciicothe felt around her neck for her mother's cross and the beautiful Masonic pendant given to her by Hiram David. They were gone, causing her heart to melt with sadness.

The days turned into weeks. Finally, word came that the governor had made a ruling concerning their fate. He had spared their lives, but Ciicothe was fined $500, Morning Star $400 and little Pete $200. These fines were to be worked off at a rate of $5 per year of service to the governor by working in the fields and doing other hard, slave-labor duties as assigned.

Ciicothe was not good at white man's math, so she was surprised when Morning Star told her that it would take her one hundred summers to pay this debt. Morning Star would only need to give eighty summers, but she could also take little Pete's debt and let him get on with his life. She and Ciicothe started laughing uncontrollably like crazy people. They knew this debt could never be paid. Little Pete looked on in panic. He believed they had lost their minds.

They were moved to a run-down, poorly built, slave cabin that had some logs falling out of place. The mud seals between the logs were dry and coming loose. The fireplace and chimney were in need of repair if they were to survive the coming winter.

Ciicothe and Morning Star were told that if they wanted to eat this winter, they would have to scrounge the harvested farm fields for any crops missed by the townspeople's harvest. They would have to compete with the rats and other scavengers. Ciicothe had agreed with Morning Star that she would gather the food in the fields and the medicine plants in the forest to supply their needs for the upcoming winter.

Morning Star would start the repairs to the ramshackle cabin offered to them as a winter shelter. She began carrying mud from the Wabash riverbank to seal the gapped openings between the logs. The guards gave them all the freedom they needed to accomplish their tasks without fear of them attempting an escape. Little Pete was being held hostage with the threat of sure death for him if they made any attempt for freedom.

Vincennes was the largest white man's town Ciicothe had ever seen. If she had not been so abused by Harrison's goons during the past weeks, she might have thought it to be a beautiful place. The town of about three hundred homes made of logs (bark or whitewashed clapboard) was built on the east bank of the Wabash River. There was a beautiful church with the remains of an old fort on the riverbank. The communal gardens were located around the perimeter towards the back of the town. There was also a great variety of fruit trees and berries.

The remains of Indian burial mounds were in every direction. Ciicothe could feel the energy of the spirits that haunted this land. White man would be horrified if the Indian people built their towns and homes on the graves of their white ancestors. But they found peace doing this to the Indian people by crushing the bones of their Indian ancestors to build homes, roads, and even churches. Some Indians had been buried for ten thousand summers, and the white men were stealing their burial belongings and using these items as their own.

Ciicothe had started her work. She was not surprised to find good amounts of dried corn, beans, hemp, and other dried foods to help them survive the winter. Nor was she surprised at the waste of the long knives. It had always been their nature (the way they lived life with their relationship to Mother Earth) to waste the animals, fruits, and the other gifts of life from the Great Good Spirit.

Ciicothe was deep into the corn patch when a rustle of stalks roused her attention. Jumping through the rows of corn was the evil Sergeant Moss. With his ear missing, he looked so funny to Ciicothe that she laughed out loud. That was a big mistake! Moss jumped into her face with a long knife pulled so fast that she could not pull away in time. His face was within inches of hers. His breath was rancid with the smell of rotted meat and whiskey. His spittle hit her face with a sting like acid. Ciicothe dropped her tote of corn as his mangy hand circled her neck. His free hand brought the knife to rest on her throat saying, "This is it for you, Indian girl."

Ciicothe could see her cross, along with the Masonic pendant given to her by Hiram, around his filthy neck. She was now on fire with anger. She lunged and pulled free, causing the knife to cut her throat. She quickly got to a six-foot-long beanpole. As she turned to use it as a spear, Sergeant Moss was poised with his long knife.

Lieutenant Bryan broke into the clearing with his pistol aimed at them. He ordered them to lower their weapons saying that the general wanted this Indian kept alive for now. There would be a right time and place to kill her.

Moss reluctantly put his knife away while giving Ciicothe an evil look and told her that his time to kill her would come soon. And when it did, he was going to cut off her head and shit in her neck hole.

Ciicothe believed every word of venom this dog had spit out. She kept the sharpened beanpole until they were out of the corn field, and would not be without a weapon in the future. She had a headband of cloth that she removed to use as a bandage around her throat to stop the bleeding from the small cut caused by the long knife. Ciicothe continued to gather any usable crops when an old, black man came into the field. This startled Ciicothe, as she had never seen a black person up close. Her weapon was ready for use.

George was an old, black man who had seen the incident of that dog Moss trying to kill Ciicothe. He was feeling very sorry for her and was ready to help her fight if his old bones would allow. Old George, a slave of Governor Harrison, had come with the general from the Berkeley Plantation on the James River, arriving in Vincennes in 1801. Old George was born a slave. He showed Ciicothe the two large notches next to three small notches on his ears to denote that he was the property of Master Harrison.

Old George didn't know his exact age or his African name, as he was a baby when he was brought to this land. He was now called a servant working for his freedom. Because this territory was free man's land, he only had to work thirty more years to be free. Old George laughed and said that he guessed he would then be one hundred twenty-eight years old, but he would be a free man!

Ciicothe laughed with old George until they cried. She liked this black man, he was the first one she had ever talked with. She knew in her heart that if all black people were like old George, it would be a good thing. Ciicothe told old George that now she was also a slave under Master Harrison. Old George reflected, he had not encountered an Indian slave before but didn't feel this was a good thing for her or anyone.

Old George helped Ciicothe harvest the remnant crops, then showed her a path that led to the ancient, well-used Buffalo Trace located behind the town. He indicated that it led to the falls on the Ohio River, which was about a three-day walk from where they were. Ciicothe had heard stories of the beautiful Ohio River with all the ancient Indian towns that once lined its banks. She had little hope that someday she might stand on the banks of the Ohio, once more a free person to enjoy the peace of that sacred place.

Ciicothe, Morning Star, and little Pete had survived a cold winter in their shack of a cabin. The food they had scavenged from the communal gardens was all but depleted. The spring plants had provided some much-needed nourishment along with a welcomed Shawnee spring elixir.

The entire Harrison family (along with their servants) had departed for North Bend on the Ohio, their family home. Old George, his family, and other slaves were part of the property moved. Ciicothe wondered if the items of the Shawnee's sacred bundle, stolen from Prophetstown on the Tippecanoe, were part of this property.

Ciicothe and the remainder of the slaves were left to work the maintenance of the mansion, to care for the three hundred acres of ground at the Grouseland Estate. The work was never ending, but the overseers who remained were kind. They treated everyone well. Ciicothe was glad that old one-ear Moss had gone with the family to North Bend. She believed she would have had to kill him before the winter ended had he remained. He was, as the Negroes said, "A piece of shit." They all believed that it was too bad that Ciicothe's tomahawk had not killed him at the cabin on the high earth.

The beautiful, spring weather they had enjoyed, changed back to cold the next day to let them know that Father Winter had not completely gone. As if the weather was not bad enough, old one-ear Moss had returned to move the remainder of the general's property, including his Indian slaves, to Ohio. He also came, with great joy, to personally deliver the news that the Great War Chief Tecumseh was dead.

Tecumseh was killed by General Harrison and his soldiers in the North British country this past October. The other Shawnee people were either massacred or had scattered to the four winds. Ciicothe could not take this news coming from Moss. As he laughed, she wanted to crush his face with a piece of firewood. But she feared retaliation towards Morning Star and little Pete. She bit her lip until blood trickled down her chin. Moss departed their cabin with one last belly laugh. There would come a time for killing this evil man.

Ciicothe's tears ran cold. She had cried for days at the news of Tecumseh's death and the massacre of the good South Wind people. She felt her heart break with each thought of Uncle Yellow Robe and her brother, Little Hawk. She now believed that she was the last of her kind. The only family she had now was Morning Star and little Pete.

Ciicothe also believed that no evil could exist on this side of the great evil spirit's domain other than that which lived in the heart of Harrison. She knew she could not let revenge fester in her heart. That was white man's trait. Revenge would consume her life if she allowed it.

On this cold, spring day, Morning Star was alone in their shack of a cabin packing the few belongings she and Ciicothe owned. Lieutenant Bryan entered the cabin and slammed the door shut. He pushed Morning Star onto the shuck bed and with his pants to his knees, forced her legs apart while holding her hands. She struggled, but it was no use, his hard manhood penetrated her body. He started to hammer his body into hers, driving his load deep into her.

Lieutenant Bryan got off of Morning Star. She was sobbing while pulling her dress down to cover her bleeding vagina. He stepped to the center of the cabin milking the remainder of his seed onto the dirt floor. He looked at Morning Star. His evil face contorted as he spit out his venomous warning. "If you tell anyone about this, I will kill that half-breed son of French's. And it will be a slow, painful death. Do you understand me, squaw?"

Morning Star nodded her head in agreement as the dog pulled up his britches. As he departed the cabin, he slammed the old door so hard it ripped off its leather hinges. Morning Star got up and squatted over the old wooden bucket, trying her best to wash his nasty seed from her body. She was in great fear that she would be cursed with this man's child. Only time would tell.

Morning Star had gone about her duties during the preparations for the move to the North Bend Estate on the Ohio. She feared that the evil seed was growing in her guts. She had the added nightmare of little Pete being killed if she were to tell anyone of this man's evil deed. She had to face the reality of this evil man's veracity at killing, knowing that just the day before he had killed a Miami Indian.

The crime was cudgeling a white man during a drunken stupor. The Indian did not know where he was, or even his own name. This Indian, crazed by having his belly full of the white man's poison (whiskey made at the Deer Creek Distillery in Cincinnati, which was owned by the evil Harrison), was accused of this murder. No matter the situation, this was an Indian, and as General Jackson said, "The only good Indian is a dead Indian." Lieutenant Bryan was the self-appointed judge, jury, and executioner.

Ciicothe was in great spirits as the line of wagons started to head southeast down the ancient Buffalo Trace. She knew the trip would be long, but she also knew the beautiful, sacred Ohio River would be there at the end of this journey, a place she longed to see. Ciicothe could not understand Morning Star's depression; she thought it might be for the loss of her beloved French, or her homeland, which she may never see again. The wagons started to roll. Ciicothe's heart began to beat with excitement.

CHAPTER 5

North Bend   1814-1822   on the Great Miami

The wagon's progress from the town of Vincennes had slowed from the relatively easy travel during the first two days of their journey. The dry section of the Buffalo Trace had made this possible. They were within a day from reaching the falls of the Ohio when the spring rains started. The cold and steady rain added to their misery. The road changed into a muddy hog lot, which caused the train of wagons to stop and dig out the ones that got stuck.

Morning Star was unusually sad and withdrawn. She had always been neat and clean before this journey, but had let her appearance go as of late. She continued to carefully watch over the care of little Pete, not straying far from his side as if she feared more for his safety. Ciicothe was worried about her beloved Morning Star's health.

The rain continued through the late afternoon of the following day. The winding road merged into a clearing from the dense forest. The clearing opened to roughly built cabins neatly lined one after another down to the banks of the most beautiful river Ciicothe had ever seen. Her heart started to beat with excitement at this wonderful site. The thought of it being the sacred Ohio intensified this feeling. A town with many larger buildings was on the other side of the river.

A large steamboat was tied to a wooden dock, this was the largest canoe Ciicothe had ever seen. The dock workers were busy offloading cargo onto the wooden docks. There was food in storage barrels along with numerous wood crates full of dry goods. Everywhere you looked people were busy.

The wagons moved slowly into the clearing near a trading post that had an area to set up camp. The coachmen wanted to get dry by waiting out this rain before starting the task of taking on their supplies.

Ciicothe wanted to have a closer look at the sacred Ohio River. Although she had been wet from the constant rain of the past two days, she wanted to soak her feet in the healing waters. As she moved in that direction, old one-ear roughly grabbed her arm almost knocking her off her feet. One-ear screamed obscenities in her ear and said that he would cut all their throats if she tried to escape. Ciicothe broke free from his filthy hands and quickly rejoined Morning Star and little Pete. She began to help set up a dry camp for them under one of the larger wagons.

Ciicothe mixed an ancient flu remedy for her family, as a nasty strain was running its course through the wagon crew, causing low spirits. The white man had brought numerous diseases and sicknesses to the native people from their homelands across the big lake. But this one was a dreadful killer for the white man, a gift from the Indians, with no cure for these greedy long knives. She would not make medicine for these evil people, for they have earned this slow, painful death.

The following day was filled with sunshine, and with it, a high lifting of spirits throughout the crew; even the slaves sang songs of happiness to God. The wagons were moved to the loading dock on the north bank where the great canoe was waiting to take on its cargo. Their excitement grew with the hope that they may ride down this beautiful river on top of this great canoe. All the activity had helped to raise Morning Star's spirits who had been sad for days after leaving Vincennes on the Wabash.

The cargo was being offloaded from the five overfilled cargo wagons. Old, evil one-ear was supervising this while Lieutenant Bryan was in an argument with a man, who appeared to Ciicothe as the chief of the great canoe. He was pointing his finger toward the wagon with the five Negro and three Indian slaves. Ciicothe was now fifteen summers old, having lived three of those summers speaking only English. She moved along the road behind the line of wagons to get closer so she could better hear this conversation.

Ciicothe made it to the first wagon, staying hidden from the roving eye of one-ear. The old canoe chief was arguing the law concerning the hauling of slaves from the slave state of Kentucky to the free state of Ohio, taking into consideration the river was in Kentucky. He was saying that he would go to jail for no one, not even General Harrison. Although Harrison called these people servants, not slaves, the chief continued to argue. He would not compromise on this issue. He would only carry the cargo in order to avoid a fight with the abolitionists in Cincinnati. Ciicothe, Morning Star, and little Pete were all heartsick not to be riding on the great canoe.

The old cargo wagon banged along the rough road leading to the Ohio country for two more days; the chains cut the flesh of their wrists. Prayers would be answered if the Rain God stayed away the two additional days before the wagon's arrival at North Bend, which would keep the roads from turning into mud again. The great canoe was expected to make the trip in only one day to the port town of Cincinnati.

Ciicothe was excited when she thought they had reached the beautiful Ohio River at the North Bend mansion, but was sad to learn that this wide, fast-moving river was the great Miami. The slave shacks on its east bank would become their homes. She was told the mansion was almost two miles away at the north bend of the Ohio River. They would not go there until settled, then only to work in the fields or help with the mansion's construction.

Two weeks had passed since their arrival, and Ciicothe and Morning Star had not yet seen the North Bend mansion. They worked their fingers to the bone to make a decent place to live out of the run down shack assigned as their home. Little Pete, when free from his assigned task, had occupied himself by playing with black slave children his age and exploring the Ohio countryside from the Miami River into the hills and surrounding valley.

Their shack of a cabin was the worst allocated for the slaves arriving from Vincennes. The cabin had been built too close to the banks of the Miami River and was prone to flooding during the rainy season, which caused the chimney to collapse to the ground last spring. The fireplace was intact, but the stack would need rebuilding before the next winter. The garden season had started for the slaves that had arrived the previous summer.

Ciicothe and Morning Star would need to play catch up, due to the short Ohio growing season, if they intended to eat this coming winter.

Ciicothe was somewhat startled when old George walked behind her and touched her arm; she felt he had the stealth of an Indian. He laughed when he saw the sharpened pole in her hands and asked if she had earned her freedom yet. Ciicothe smiled and replied that she only had ninety-eight summers left to give the old general, then she would be free.

Old George wanted Ciicothe to walk with him; this would be her first look at the North Bend mansion overlooking the beautiful Ohio River. He told Ciicothe that they were, at present, adding two wings onto the mansion to make a total of sixteen rooms. It would have a formal great room, entrance foyer, and a large kitchen; all with natural hardwood floors, the elegance befitting a retired general.

The mansion faced south and stood two hundred ninety yards from the banks of the beautiful Ohio. The grounds were lush with tall, virgin timber of locust, oak, evergreen, maple, catalpa, buckeye, and shagbark hickory. A formal garden was planted with fruit trees, berries, and other crops to sustain the family's needs.

The farm sat on 3,000 acres and had freshwater springs in the hills above the mansion. Gravity forced the water needs to the family, which had ten children and four adults. Plumbing, lighting, and heating systems installed at the estate were made in the most modern manner of the time. Springs also brought water for irrigation of all the garden and lawn requirements, which allowed for a lush landscape, and beautiful plants and trees.

Ciicothe asked old George where he lived, as she had not seen him in slave town. George laughed and pointed towards a grouping of barns with outside storage buildings and an attached cabin smokehouse. Next to these buildings were quarters for George and his family, which had two rooms that were comfortable compared to the shacks at slave town.

George's housing allowed him to take care of the needs of the Harrison family at the mansion on an immediate basis. His wife and children were also involved in taking care of the Harrison family. Their jobs included gathering firewood, chamber pot emptying, cleaning, food preparation and any other needs the family had. All the Harrison family was required to do was ring the service bell.

George pointed to the east, indicating the town of Cincinnati (or "Pork Polis" as some people called it), which was eighteen miles in that direction. The expansion of the flat boat business had exploded in the past year. The shipping of flour, pork, whiskey, and other crops to New Orleans, with commerce at ports all along the great rivers, made Cincinnati one of the most important ports on the river.

The conversation with George was informative and pleasant. Ciicothe learned valuable knowledge that would help her survive her captivity. Then a serious change transformed the usually jolly, old, black man. He told her of his sorrow of the death of the great Chief Tecumseh. Then, almost in a whisper, he cautioned Ciicothe of the general's men having an unbridled lust to rape the slave women, and the general would not attempt to stop them.

Ciicothe stopped him because she did not understand this word "rape" or what danger it posed to Morning Star and herself. Old George realized he was talking to a child in an adult situation. Mayhap the appearance of her burns, damaged eye, and other scars had helped to keep the general's dogs off her, but Morning Star was in great danger.

Old George knew the danger firsthand with his seventeen-year-old daughter birthing his two grandchildren; they were products of the night visits by the hooded men. There was nothing he could do to stop them; they kept him in fear of death for his family. George reluctantly pulled up his shirt to reveal a long scar inflicted by Harrison's goons when he first opposed their rapes. Ciicothe could feel his pain and anguish of not being able to do anything. The general did nothing to stop this treatment because it added to his slave wealth of selling the excess children in the slave market of Kentucky.

Ciicothe returned to their cabin after a ten hour day of working the farm fields at the mansion. She was exhausted, but had many more hours of work to help them get out of their predicament. She saw Morning Star in their small garden laughing at the antics of little Pete, who was now five summers old and full of piss and vinegar. The laughter was the first she had heard from Morning Star in months; it was good to hear.

Nightfall was rapidly approaching, so Ciicothe joined in the work. While they hoed the tender, young crops, Ciicothe relayed the information she had gotten from old George. When she got to the part about the night goons raping the slaves, Morning Star's face turned white as if she had seen a ghost. Her laughter was gone; she could have done without reliving the story of that crime at the cabin in Vincennes. At this point, Morning Star felt Ciicothe needed to know the truth. If she didn't tell her, she would soon find out when the growth of the child started to show in her belly.

Ciicothe's anger burned in her gut. She knew the day would come when the rapist dogs would see she was becoming a young woman ready to breed. She believed her appearance would no longer stop the general's goons. She would not become another woman with child to add to the general's wealth of slaves, nor to her misery.

Morning Star, Ciicothe, and little Pete had survived one more winter in captivity. They added a new person to the slave numbers on the day of the man Jesus' birth. The Harrison family saw this as a particularly good omen and made certain there was extra food provided for the Bethlehem Indian shack (which is what the Harrison family started calling their cabin). The general's family named the baby girl Mary. Ciicothe and Morning Star called her Blue Turtle Eyes. They knew she would be a significant person in all of their lives. But for now, she was only a baby needing milk from her mother.

The years had come and gone quickly. The hard work of the farm life kept them occupied by the harvesting, processing, and replanting of the gardens for a new season of work. Ciicothe was now nineteen summers old. She had changed from a scrawny, little girl into a beautiful, young woman. With the aging process, came a healing of the burn scars that are now partly hidden by her long, raven-black hair. Her right eye was now sightless, yet her internal sight was stronger than ever. She had dreams of the old, one-eyed shaman, Tenskwatawa, and how he survived with only one good eye.

Ciicothe and her extended family were flooded out of their shack by the great Miami during the first two springs. The birth of Mary changed their standing in the slave ranks. The support for them by the Harrison family improved. There was an increased share of food and clothing, and they had assistance with building a new cabin on higher ground with a loft for a warm sleeping room during the cold Ohio winters. Ciicothe had become very fond of Mrs. Anna, the general's wife, as she always showed her good heart for Morning Star, little Pete, and Mary. Mrs. Anna was most likely the reason for the improved station in their lives as slaves.

The past winter of 1818-1819 had been a season of much sickness. The slave community had learned of Ciicothe's abilities as a Shawnee healer. She welcomed the chance to help the other slaves with her knowledge of the ancient cures through the use of native medicines.

The sickness had overcome the townspeople of Cincinnati. The Harrison family was not spared illness that winter. John Scot was near death by the time Mrs. Anna humbled herself to come to the Indian cabin. She begged for Ciicothe's help, saying that she had learned from old George the reason the slaves remained healthy while the white community fell dead to the sickness or lay weak from the fever for weeks.

Ciicothe pondered this request because that meant she would be helping the people that massacred her family; she now had life or death control over them. *If I refuse, would the better treatment of receiving extra food, clothing, a new cabin, and the other positive changes stop?* Ciicothe prayed on it and got her answer.

Ciicothe was very concerned by the thought of the white man's greed. *If they had my knowledge of the old Indian remedies, what would become of them?* With her help, the Harrison family survived the flu. John Scot had recovered by the spring planting.

Upon the new season of hunting the fall crop of medicine plants and roots, Ciicothe was not alone. The general had placed a trainee with her so he could learn the types of plants harvested and the sicknesses that her remedies cured. She knew her abilities were the only advantage she had over this evil master; it may even be the only ticket out of this hell.

The general was elected as an Ohio senator and was now traveling between North Bend and the new state capital in Columbus (old Franklinton). Ciicothe knew he ordered the trainee to learn the secrets of the Shawnee medicines. Harrison wanted her to meet with the apothecaries in Cincinnati to sell these old remedies, which would allow him to profit from God's gifts given to the good South Wind people.

Ciicothe was only a child when Uncle Yellow Robe and Tall Walker Woman worked to pass on the magic of their people's medicines. There was also a dark side of the shaman's craft passed on to her; that of the deadly poisons that killed as quickly as the medicines cured. She remembered that the use of these poisons was to quickly kill deer and small game, a great help for the hunters. The poisons were also used to make a minor wound on an enemy grow into a deadly infection that would kill long after the battlefield action had ended.

The young man assigned to study the process of making the native Indian medicines was very intelligent and a quick study. His name was William Merrell and was near Ciicothe's age. She liked him and was learning from him as well as teaching him. He was planning to go east to Hamilton College the following year and was excited to learn as much as he could from Ciicothe's skills.

William wanted to become a pharmacist, to be able to help all people. Ciicothe thought he had a good heart and was one of the kindest white people she had known, with the exception of Hiram. Ciicothe was sad the following year when her friend William departed for college. She felt a tinge of love for this white man, she would miss him.

The man now assigned to follow Ciicothe through the development of the medicines was rude. His father was on the war campaign with Harrison to exterminate her people; he had developed a real hatred for Indians. She had made her mind up not to share any more of the process of the medicines with him. Ciicothe had set a goal to either have this man replaced or to let him try some tick-weed poison tea. That brew would rid her of this nasty human forever. But she knew that if her actions angered the old general her life would change for the worst.

Ciicothe had suffered through the fall gathering season. The medicines were prepared and stored. She had shared very little knowledge with Jake. He was an evil man, who was only there to steal the secrets and make a profit from her people's gift. She truly missed William, an honest, kind man who shared as much knowledge as he had taken away. He had helped Ciicothe improve the medicines.

The general was now home from the Ohio state house. The once generous gifts of extra clothing, food, and protection from the hooded men's rampages at night to rape the slave women were gone. Old George gained two more grandchildren from his young daughters, who had never been with men voluntarily. Other slave women also contributed to the slave population. The older children were sold at the Maysville, Kentucky slave auction on the courthouse square. People were sold on the streets to the highest bidder like cattle.

Ciicothe knew she needed to do something to protect her family. The crude weapons she made could do little to stop an aggressive man with sex on his mind. She began to work on a poison poultice. The problem was how to make it effective enough when applied to the man trying to have sex without killing him. A generous swipe of this love potion and sex would be the last thing on his mind.

In order not to poison the person applying this mess onto the working sex organs of the man, all precautions would need to be taken. Ciicothe worked for weeks creating gloves from the gut of a butchered hog to protect her hands so she could spread the noxious mixture safely. The time had come to tell Morning Star how to use the rape repellant.

The flurry of activity concerning the last of the harvest, along with the preparation of food for the winter, was taking its toll on the slave population. The critical nature of food storage had eased somewhat due to the rapid growth of the city of Cincinnati. The flatboat business had expanded, making this transportation port the busiest on the Ohio River with the shipping of farm products, pork, and whiskey as far south as New Orleans.

Ciicothe had gone on two transport trips (eighteen miles to Cincinnati) to deliver the farm products that were in excess of the Harrison family's needs. Harrison was making a profit produced from the backs of the hard work of the North Bend slaves. The shocking news in the early winter of 1821 was that a slave had earned his freedom; old Jack Butler was now a free man after only fourteen years.

Jack enjoyed freedom for a short time once before when he escaped slavery. However, he was captured and resold into service to the general. Now, he was free at last. Mayhap there was hope for Ciicothe and her family. The word amongst the other slaves was that Ohio slavery laws were forcing the general's hand. As of now, they could only look forward to the dreams of freedom that occupied their nights.

Morning Star, little Pete, and Ciicothe had settled in on this cold, snow-filled, bleak night. The weather was so severe on this night in late January that Morning Star would stay with the cabin fireplace the first half of the night stoking the fire and not banking it as normal. This would allow Ciicothe, little Pete and Blue Turtle Eyes a warm bed in the loft where most of the cabin warmth gathered.

Ciicothe had fallen into a deep sleep. She dreamed of the good times that could have been at Prophetstown on the Tippecanoe River and of the friendship that could have been with the white man, had greed not consumed their souls. She was ripped from her peaceful sleep by a muffled sound from the lower floor of the cabin. She moved quickly down the ladder from the loft.

In the light from the roaring fireplace, Ciicothe saw a hooded man with his britches down on top of Morning Star trying to drive his manhood into her. Ciicothe jumped the remainder of the distance from the loft, twisting her ankle. The hooded man did not see or hear anything, his mind was now on his swollen manhood and only thinking of what he wanted to do with it.

Ciicothe quickly put on the hog-gut gloves, then located the wooden bucket full of the poison; she didn't hesitate to get a huge handful of this noxious brew. She approached him from behind and spread the poison around the area of his manhood and into the depths of his anal canal. He released his chokehold from Morning Star's throat as he screamed in agony. She finished with him by putting the remainder of the poison from her gloved hand into his eyes.

The hooded man spun out of control and hit the side of Ciicothe's head with a glancing blow. He got up and bolted for the door. His deflated manhood was dripping blood from the cutting action of the buckeye shells. He hit the door of the cabin in a dead run, most likely looking for some water to cool his burning balls; that is, if he could see to find water.

Ciicothe locked the door and blocked it with their wooden table. She didn't think he would return, but all the screaming may have alerted some of his thug friends. Ciicothe worked to calm Morning Star and the children as she kept the fire going. She knew there would be hell to come when Harrison learned of the injuries to this white man. Ciicothe knew this man would not be looking for a woman for a long time.

The body of the dead rapist was found on the frozen banks of the great Miami. When the hood was removed, the face of the evil Jake was revealed. Ciicothe was not surprised. His eyes were clawed from their sockets, and his britches were still at his ankles exposing his balls, which were a mangled mess. He obviously could not get through the ice to get to the cooling relief of the water below. He died the death that he earned.

Ciicothe hid the poison and the hog-gut gloves. She knew Harrison's thugs would search each cabin. At present, they were confused as to how Jake had died. It was just a matter of time before the goons would figure it out. Ciicothe knew the time was at hand, they had to escape this slave prison.

The general was very upset about this murder on his property. Due to his relationship with Jake's father, a hero of Tippecanoe, he vowed to solve this mystery. Ciicothe knew he was most likely more concerned with his income of slave babies being curtailed. With the fear of the same death happening to his other breeders, caution was their watchword. Not one rapist wanted to test the will of the slaves to use this poison on the next man bold enough to chance a night visit to any of the cabins.

Ciicothe and her family had tried for months to stay out of the light of the investigation into the death of Jake. Just as they thought the witch hunt was over, Jake's father got involved bringing the wrath of God down on the Indians' cabin. Jake's father, having an informant within the slave ranks, believed he could go to the general with evidence for holding court to execute the Indian that murdered his son.

The day started out as normal, Ciicothe went to work in the farm fields.

She used this cover to continue hiding some needed supplies in a wooded area near the Miami River heading south towards the mouth where it joined the beautiful Ohio River (spaylaywitheepi). She heard screaming coming from the Indian cabin. As she ran in that direction, she saw Morning Star laying on the ground crying.

Little Pete had grown into a strapping young man of thirteen summers old and was lying motionless on the ground next to Morning Star. Ciicothe quickly saw that Pete was alive, but just knocked out of his senses and had an open wound on his head. Morning Star could only say, "Blue Turtle Eyes" over and over; she seemed to have lost her mind. Ciicothe realized that her actions had brought this new hell on her family and had no possible way to correct the situation.

Ciicothe knew it was time to go. Blue Turtle Eyes had been gone for two days. The little girl was now seven summers old and prime meat for the slave auction. Ciicothe was preparing for their escape, while Morning Star cried the entire time. Ciicothe thought Morning Star might have lost her mind completely; sometimes she would cry out "Sheltowee" which translated Big Turtle. Ciicothe could make no sense of what Morning Star was trying to say. She attempted to speak with her to plan their escape, but Morning Star was adamant that she could not leave without Blue Turtle Eyes.

The next day, Ciicothe awoke to little Pete's frantic voice. The morning light was coming through the open door. Pete struggled to tell her something about his mother. He calmed himself long enough to say that she had left the cabin with the poison, and was heading towards the Harrison Estate.

By the time Ciicothe had pulled herself together and climbed the hill to the back of the mansion, her worst fear had occurred. Morning Star was lying dead five feet from the rear steps of the mansion. The bucket of poison was next to her outstretched arm, and the hog-gut gloves were on her hands. One-ear Moss was standing over Pete. The gun used to crack Pete's skull was now leveled at his head. Pete's hands were holding the flow of blood from a severe scalp wound.

As Ciicothe approached, old one-ear shifted the focus of his weapon onto her. He saw the fire burning in her eyes, as well as the makeshift weapon she intended to use. The good-hearted Mrs. Anna came to the porch just in time. She probably saved a life that day. One-ear should thank God that he had gotten a reprieve. Ciicothe believed that she had caused this tragedy to her family and she had opened the raw evil of this place. If not for the intervention of Harrison's wife Anna, she and little Pete would also be dead.

The following day Ciicothe stood by the funeral fire on the banks of the Great Miami River. Little Pete had recovered from his scalp wound, but his heart would never heal from the loss of his mother. The slaves had assembled all praying for Morning Star and, in part, themselves. By her actions and death, Morning Star had taken the punishment for Jake's murder. His family's bloodlust was satisfied with this result, and they moved on. Ciicothe knew in her heart that the general was not pleased, and would want more bloodshed. She knew she must move on: either by leaving this place or by having her own funeral fire.

Ciicothe talked with old George. She learned that Blue Turtle Eyes was gone, most likely at the slave auction in Maysville, Kentucky. Ciicothe confided in George of her plan to escape. She trusted him and needed his help. She asked him to help her retrieve the sacred bundle items stolen from Prophetstown. George had unfettered access to the mansion, he could guide her to the place where she could recover her tribe's property.

Ciicothe was prepared to leave. George informed her of the location of the sacred bundle items in the mansion. Little Pete was hiding in the woods with the food, medicines, and other needed gear packed and ready to go, with part of the supplies (intended to feed three) to be abandoned if need be. The fires in the slave cabins were set by Ciicothe as a distraction. The large storage barn was also set ablaze. Stationed at the mansion, she was ready to get her property as soon as the alarm raised the mansion's occupants. She could not believe her good fortune.

Screams were coming from every direction, along with overflowing panic. Everyone was running with wooden buckets to the fire's glow at the crest of the hill towards the slave shacks. Ciicothe entered the mansion. Using old George's directions, she quickly found what she came for. Still wrapped in its ancient white buffalo hide was the sacred property of the South Wind people.

Ciicothe started to exit when a bundle of letters on the top of an old desk caught her eye. She knew what she needed to do. She would return some of the pain to Harrison by taking something valuable of his. The tied bundle of letters and documents were clutched in her hands as she reunited with little Pete at his hiding place. They were set to taste freedom for the first time in eleven years.

CHAPTER 6

Frog Town   May 1963   on the Ohio

The haze in the living room at Grandma Lu's small, frame house on Ninth Street was stifling. The distinct smell of kinnikinnick smoke, along with hellish screeching from the front of the house, brought me back to reality. The crazy screaming out on the front sidewalk was Grandma Lu. She had the working end of her broom making contact with my main man Magoo's big behind.

Now Magoo was only here to see how I was doing like a good road dog should. But Grandma Lu was telling him to move his black behind on down the street. I was too broke up and scared of Grandma Lu to come to his aid. Magoo was on his own, like a ruptured goose on the loose in a hail storm and would have to catch hell for my dumb-ass miscalculation for a short time longer. He went on his merry way.

The snoring from Grandma Wick made me sleepy. It was time for a good nap, but Grandma Lu had other plans for the remainder of my day. She intended to get my butt up and working. You see work could somehow heal you faster than laying on your dead ass. But first, Grandma Lu had some stinky Indian elixir for me to take.

You might think I don't know shit from shin-o-la about Indian medicines, but you would be wrong. This crap Grandma Lu was trying to stuff down my cakehole was a laxative. The old grandmas' belief was to keep the bottom end open and the top half would take care of itself. You might think this was a good theory, but after pooping out all of your energy, you soon would have no will to fight. This was a good Indian trick to weaken their enemy, then cut off body parts and burn the rest in the campfire, game over.

You would be right in thinking Grandma Lu would win this war of the wills. I am now butt-hugging the porcelain convenience for the fourth time today. Between cutting firewood, and any other job she put on my aching back, running to the crapper and shooting liquid mud out of my bunghole was only a short break from work.

I hobbled my way back to school and finished the year under much duress. I couldn't help but think about the story Grandma Wick had started. With summer coming on, I should be on the run like a one-winged fly. I could have eased on down the road that summer and missed out on the most incredible story of my life. But somehow, the urgency of me learning the remainder of our family's secret history was powerful. I found myself being compelled by a hidden spirit to return to my grandmas' house.

Grandma Lu met me at the door with her usual lovely greeting, "What the hell are you doing back here? Have you jumped into another sand pit breaking your dumb ass again?" I was trying to think of a good comeback, but the only thing I could visualize was a major dose of her elixir being forced down my throat.

"Hi Grandma Lu, I love you too. I came to talk with Grandma Wick about our Indian heritage," was all I was able to say before Grandma Lu turned to walk to her kitchen.

She mumbled something about crazy Indian stories and said, "The next thing you know Grandma Wick will have you climbing the cliffs back of Ironton looking for the tomb of Tecumseh." That statement got my attention!

Grandma Lu walked back into the living room, looked at me, and said, "I can tell you the way the damned Indians could have defeated the white man, with lawyers. Yes, a whole butt-load of dirty, damn lawyers. If the Indians had lawyers they would be rich today!" Then she turned and went back to her kitchen, grunting about her satisfaction of her prophetic statement.

Now I had learned Ohio history in school, and of the numerous Indian tribes that lived in Ohio for over 15,000 years (the Shawnee, Wyandot, Delaware, and Miami), and how not a single tribe existed in this state now. No, not one solitary full-blooded Indian, just us half-breeds remain. We were what was left behind to tell the story, and we sure wished they had hired some damn, dirty-dog lawyers four hundred years ago.

Grandma Wick was in the process of loading her long-stemmed, stone, smoking pipe with some fresh kinnikinnick. She looked at me as the fire from her kitchen match started the smoke to boil from the bowl of her ancient, stone pipe. To help prompt her memory, she asked me what river Ciicothe was living on when the story ended. I should have not been surprised at how important the rivers were in the lives of all people, most importantly the Indian tribes.

Grandma Wick looked up into the air, paused for several minutes as if to pull her thoughts from someplace in space, while the smoke from her long-stemmed, stone Shawnee pipe started to burn my eyes. Grandma Wick, in a hypnotic, musical language, chanted what I believed to be a Shawnee prayer. She ended the prayer with tears in her eyes, then resumed her story.

CHAPTER 7

The Underground Railroad 1822-1823 on the Scioto River

Ciicothe and little Pete traveled south where the great Miami entered the Ohio. The rivers combined their strengths at this junction and turned west to join the father of all rivers, the Mississippi. Ciicothe knew she must go east, but they had departed North Bend leaving a false trail to the north, mayhap fooling the angry mob looking for them. She knew a reward would be offered for the recovery of the general's property, and his legion of goons would not give up. Harrison was a powerful man with an enormous influence in the Ohio country; he would never stop searching for them.

They traveled east on the banks of the Ohio. Ciicothe was surprised to see the town of Cincinnati in the distance; their pace was much faster than she had thought. They continued to run along the bank of the old Ohio River path. She did not want to camp on this side of the town, but instead wished to use the darkness of the setting sun to go through the busy dock section. She prayed this would allow them to pass through without detection, as the general had men working throughout this place that could recognize her.

Ciicothe was amazed at their progress; the dock workers paid little to no attention to them. She and little Pete were both burdened with two full packs of food, along with the other things needed to survive their journey. She had not looked through the bundle of the general's property nor the sacred items of the Shawnee people recovered from the North Bend mansion. These things made her tote bags heavy, which slowed her progress through the maze of wagons that were stacked full of dry goods being loaded onto the flatboats.

They were now on the trail that passed adjacently to the last of the cargo on the east side of town. Ciicothe felt a bit of relief in her heart to see the river road just a short walking distance from them. She knew this would give them the cover of the forest along the Ohio River road and would allow for a little more safety from detection.

Little Pete and Ciicothe had just rounded the last of the dry goods when Harrison's wagon boss Ichabod Wilson (a large, surly man) recognized them. He knew Ciicothe from the wagon trip from the falls of the Ohio. He was a man who would try to stop them. Before she could react, Ichabod ran towards them and grabbed little Pete by the arm, stopping him so abruptly that his loaded down tote bags went sailing through the air. Having seen this, her anger grew instantly, like an inferno of rage.

Ciicothe dropped all of her load except the tote with the ancient, stone cup. She clutched the leather straps in both hands. While running towards the three-hundred-pound man, she began swinging the bag over her head. The tote bag with the stone cup connected at the base of the big man's skull. There was a sound like a dry gourd busting open. All of the life instantly departed the eyes of Ichabod and he lost his grip on little Pete's arm.

The only sound Ciicothe could hear was that of this big man gagging on his own blood, causing him to lose his mud. A massive wet fart followed him to the ground as he hit face first, knocking over several barrels in the process. Two more of Harrison's men came running at the sound of the scuffle. Ciicothe helped gather little Pete's totes and moved quickly to retrieve the bags she had dropped. She believed they would be followed on the river road and captured; her mind was spinning.

Ciicothe felt faint from exhaustion (caused by the combination of the fight as well as the other events of the day) when she saw a haze in the distance. A figure appeared that resembled Morning Star. It seemed as if she was guiding them away from the river road towards a group of loaded wagons.

Mayhap it was a fresh breeze that had caused the flap of the hide tarp to move, or could it have been *Morning Star's* ghost that led us to this wagon? Ciicothe thanked God and accepted the guidance as the apparition vanished. She went to the wagon, lifted the tarp, and motioned little Pete to follow. They climbed in with the thought of only hiding temporarily from the angry men running down the river road.

It felt as if they had been in the wagon for hours when in reality only about twenty minutes had elapsed. Ciicothe heard talking next to them. The horses started to buck at the activity. One of the men began to tie down the tarp covering the cargo, while the second man got on board preparing to control the team of horses. As soon as the man completed his task of tying down the load, he boarded the wagon. They started down the Ohio River road at a speed indicating that time was not on their side.

Ciicothe could not make out the conversation over the noise from the road. Through a crack in the wagon's sideboards, she could see a group of men searching the riverbank. One of the searchers came to the side of the road flagging them to stop. The man introduced himself as the general's foreman from the Deer Creek Whiskey Distillery. He explained that they were looking for a murderer.

The man on the wagon introduced himself as Reverend John Rankin and said he was taking winter supplies to his property in Ripley, Ohio. He then stated that he had seen no travelers on this part of the river road and that his load had been secured before they departed Cincinnati. Reverend Rankin complained that daylight was burning and was given the go-ahead to continue. The noise the wagons created as they began to roll allowed Ciicothe to breathe again, and her heartbeat return to normal.

The rough wagon ride jarred their bones for three hours. Every joint in Ciicothe's body ached, and the hunger in her gut was intense. She and little Pete had not eaten since the day before their escape from North Bend. The driver brought the wagon to a halt. Ciicothe thought they were stopping for the night, as the darkness had closed in so completely that she could no longer see through the crack in the sideboards.

As Ciicothe's eyes were adjusting to the limited light, an oil lantern was lit next to the wagon that temporarily blinded her. When her eyes became adapted to the change of light, she could see that they were in a barn. The men were tending to their horse team, bedding and feeding them for the night. She could hear their conversation. They wanted to wait until morning to offload the cargo. She thought that at last they would have a little luck. The lantern was extinguished, and the two voices faded into the night. The horses could be heard as they munched on their hay.

Ciicothe knew she must find something for them to eat. The pemmican in their bags would do if they could not find anything in the wagon that would give them more nourishment. After a quick look in the wagon, she could see all the stores were sealed in barrels or wooden boxes. They settled for the food in their bags brought from North Bend. Ciicothe wanted to leave this place but would have to wait until dawn to find her way to the river road. She found an empty stall with hay, and they settled in for a good night's rest.

Ciicothe awoke to the sound of a gun being cocked. As she opened her eyes, she saw that she was looking into the barrel of a Kentucky long gun; she woke little Pete. They were ordered to get up and walk outside towards a little house on a small hill. The mist of the cool, fall morning was slowly burning off when the Reverend John Rankin stepped out onto his front porch. He looked surprised at the site of the scrawny, teenage, half-breed boy with an Indian woman who had scars on her face. Their hair was matted with hay and horse manure.

The Reverend Rankin calmed the situation like that of a man with high stature, comparable to a great chief. He allowed the two the needed time to clean up, then invited them into his home to eat with him and his family. The kindness of this white man surprised Ciicothe. She did not know whether or not to trust him, as just the evening before she was forced to kill an evil, white man to protect her family. This kind man listened to her story and gave her ideas to help them.

The Reverend Rankin was an abolitionist, a word that was not in Ciicothe's vocabulary. As the reverend continued, he voiced his hatred of slavery and for the people who traded in the human misery of others. He promised Ciicothe his help to escape her bondage of personal hell by the use of the Underground Railroad.

The weeks passed by quickly at the Reverend Rankin's home. He advised Ciicothe to change her name. He explained that by taking an English name, they could better assimilate her into white society. With his wife's help, Ciicothe was able to change her appearance with new clothing. The use of a conservative head bonnet helped hide her long, black hair and damaged face. Ciicothe had a more difficult time choosing her new name. At this moment, she could not appreciate the significance of this needed change. But with time, she would see how it could save her life during her travels in the Underground Railroad and her new life in the free world.

Reverend Rankin knew the power of the old general and his connections in the Ohio Statehouse. He saw the political importance of the letters and documents taken from North Bend. The idea of converting the native population into slaves and deporting or killing off the black slaves was not a new concept, and here was documentation of this from leaders of this state and the nation. These were critical documents to have in one's possession. The information they contained only reinforced Reverend Rankin's goals as an ardent abolitionist in setting his mission for human rights to abolish all slavery in this country.

Ciicothe walked to the banks of the Ohio River and prayed for inspiration. The selection of a white man's name had tormented her for days. She looked into the swirling waters and at the willows on the banks, which was a source of pain relief for the South Wind people for thousands of years. She also saw the reeds and rushes along the banks that help hold the soil from the brutal flow of the mighty river. She had her name! She would become Willow Reed.

The time had come for Willow and little Pete to depart their hiding place with the Reverend Rankin; danger was close at hand. They were too close to Cincinnati and the general's thugs. Information received by Reverend Rankin indicated that they needed to move on. Willow (with her new name and look) headed east with little Pete to the farm of Will Brand located on the Scioto River. The ground had frozen; travel would be rough but fast with no mud to contend with.

Willow prayed with Reverend Rankin before departing. She had asked for forgiveness for the evil people she had been forced to kill. They prayed for the freedom of all God's people, and she added a silent prayer to see her new friend Reverend Rankin again someday soon.

Willow and little Pete arrived at the farm of Will Brand on the banks of the old Scioto River, which flowed from the northern Ohio country to the south joining the beautiful Ohio River. Willow remembered the stories of the ancient Shawnee towns of Chillicothe, Pique, Eskippakithiki, and Kispoko, which followed the flow of this sacred river. They all had wigwam ninety feet long, and great council houses of one hundred twenty feet long. The happy South Wind people had lived in safety, enjoying the gifts of Mother Earth from the Great Good Spirit.

Will Brand and his family embraced Willow and little Pete as if they were long-lost family members. They opened their home to them with a warmth Willow had never known. She and little Pete were given a private bedroom, something she had never experienced. The kitchen was a grand gathering place for all of the family, and the food was delicious. The work required of Willow and little Pete was limited to the collection of firewood for the cookstove and fireplaces.

Willow had the most extraordinary winter of her life. They celebrated the Christmas holiday with a family that truly prayed with their hearts, not just their mouths. It gave her a rebirth of her Christian teachings from Uncle Yellow Robe's Bible, restoring her faith that some white men still lived by the words of the man Jesus. Nor were they all consumed by greed.

Willow's workload was doubled during the spring planting season. Little Pete had evolved into a fine young man at fourteen summers old. He could no longer be called little. He was an excellent worker and had a jolly attitude towards life. He showed little sadness at the tragic events of his short life. Everyone he met liked him. Willow was very content here but knew this was only temporary lodging. The time would soon come for them to move further east.

The summer and fall quickly passed. With sadness in his heart, Will Brand told Willow the time had come for them to leave due to the rumblings of danger coming from the west. The early freeze of the Scioto River would allow them to cross over going east. His good friend, a Masonic Brother, would be their contact for a safe-house. He told them his Masonic Brother had a trading post on the Ohio and he could give them jobs. Willow was shocked to hear the new contact's name. She had to ask Will to repeat himself. "Hiram David," Will said with some curiosity.

Willow went to the bundle of sacred items and retrieved the Masonic emblem given to her by Hiram. She had recovered it from the North Bend mansion. Will was gap-mouthed as he listened to her incredible story. He had heard some of the details of Hiram's war efforts at Tippecanoe with his subsequent rescue from the grave by a young Indian child but did not realize the general's thugs had put him in this grave with two dead Masonic Brothers.

Willow's excitement for a reunion with Hiram David consumed her thoughts as they crossed the frozen Scioto River on this cold December morning. The journey was only forty-eight miles to the east. The trip would take a full day due to the undeveloped roads and limited bridges crossing the numerous streams between the Scioto River and the town of South Point, Ohio.

Willow had time on this trip to consider the significance of the documents and letters taken by her from the North Bend mansion. There was also a sum of paper bank notes and gold in which she tried to give to Will Brand. He said there was too much blood on Harrison's money and he would have none of it. Because they were correspondence from presidents, governors, and other generals with information concerning the treatment of the Indian populations, the letters were the most interesting to her. Most of them were marked "private" or "keep close to the vest."

There were instructions for death teams of militia to kill Indians and slaughter white settlers. With these murders being blamed on the Indians, the frontier population kept a genuine fear and hate of the native people. There were also instructions on the methods of the control of the Indians' treaty lands, along with ways to control the food supply, hunting, waterways, and eventual extermination through smallpox or other diseases. The result of all these actions was the theft of all the Indian land as well as the final extermination of all the tribes.

Willow was startled back to the present when the wagon became stuck in the marshy soil of the road along the Ohio River. The open, bottom land at the base of the hills provided easy travel with the frozen marsh for the first forty miles. Now their luck had run out on this last eight-mile run. They offloaded the wagon of people and cargo. They pushed with no luck, the wagon would not budge. They had seen several smoke plumes from cabins in the distance; the driver set out to get help. Willow and Pete started a fire. A light snow began to fall, which increased the bone chill they all had.

It seemed to Willow that they had been traveling for hours since having gotten the buckboard wagon unstuck. The help of several goodhearted, iron furnace workers ensured that they would not freeze on this snowy night. They passed through a densely populated area called Frog Town. There was some construction of numerous ironworks in various stages of completion, and other large buildings being built. Willow's thoughts were interrupted as the wagon came to a stop. Willow looked up to see a large, rough-hewn sign that read David and Sons General Store. She and Pete were home!

CHAPTER 8

The General Store Secrets   South Point   1824-1829   on the Ohio

The night chill had set in completely with the snow falling at a blinding pace. They sat as if frozen on the wagon seat. A tall man emerged from the first, and largest, of three cabins carrying an oil lantern in his left hand, and a long gun in his right. The man cautiously approached the wagon, followed by two young boys. When the light was close enough to recognize the occupants, Hiram almost dropped his lantern. All he could say was, "Ciicothe," over and over and over.

In the warmth of the largest of the three cabins, the reunion was glorious. Willow brought Hiram up to date with the tragic stories of her life as a slave on the Wabash and Miami Rivers. She described the gracious care given by Reverend Rankin and the Brand family on the Scioto River.

Hiram was heartbroken to learn of the deaths of his Masonic Brother, French and his wife, Morning Star. Hiram's anger at the evil people that caused these deaths could not be contained. He did not consider himself a vengeful man, yet someone must pay for these tragedies. He vowed on his Masonic oath to exact revenge.

Hiram described his journey to the southern Ohio hill country. He met his beloved wife, Martha, in the small community of Hanging Rock about four miles to the west of South Point. Joseph, his first-born son, was now ten years old. Isaac, born two years later, was eight. The boys were named in honor of his murdered Masonic Brothers buried in the ground in Indiana.

Beth, his beloved little girl, died at birth with their mother Martha, who had contracted the flu during the epidemic of 1819. Willow was heartbroken that she didn't have the chance to save Hiram's wife, as she was a slave working to heal the Harrison family during this epidemic.

The conversation slowed; they were exhausted from the journey and wonderful reunion. Willow and Pete were each given a private bedroom. The cabin they were to stay in overnight had two bedrooms, a large living room with a separate kitchen, and two fireplaces. One fireplace was in the kitchen for cooking and a larger one in the living area for heating the house. The wagon driver was to be bedded in the vacant cabin at the end of the row of modest lodgings where he could warm himself by the fireplace and have his dinner. Hiram promised to find Willow and Pete permanent housing in the morning.

The following morning Willow prepared a breakfast fit for a king, all to Hiram's delight. After they had eaten, they went a short distance to the David and Sons General Store. Willow was astonished at the number of goods in one place. They had all types of food, dry goods, and hardware. The snow that accumulated overnight would slow the number of customers for this day's trade, which would give them the blessing of more time to catch up on the events of their eleven years of separation.

Hiram revealed his plan to move his old Indian helper, Thomas, into the small cabin at the end of the property. Thomas occupied the middle cabin that had been his home since his arrival here in 1815. This cabin located next to Hiram's house had a full kitchen and plenty of room; it would better fit Ciicothe's needs.

Hiram had rescued old Thomas from the hangman's noose, finding him near death and mostly blind. He and Martha doctored this poor, Christian Indian, who had one foot in the grave. They worked for several weeks to save this wretch for an unfinished, God-given mission.

Several times that day, Hiram made the mistake of using Willow's Indian name, Ciicothe. He did not need to be reminded of the importance of not using her Indian name, as this could get them all killed. The permanent part in his hair from a musket round was a constant reminder of this danger. "Oh, your name is Willow now. Sorry, I keep forgetting." Just as

Hiram was clearing up his mistake concerning Willow's new name, the door opened. In walked an old Indian wrapped in a faded yellow robe.

Willow could not believe her eyes! Her jaw was hanging slack, her mouth gaped open. There was no mistaking this man. It was her Uncle Yellow Robe! Willow rushed to meet her beloved uncle as he staggered across the rough-hewn wood floor. She wrapped her arms around him as he pulled back from her.

Hiram quickly spoke, "Willow, old Thomas is nearly blind. Talk to him so he can remember your voice." As Willow spoke, her old uncle's head began to swivel on his neck. He immediately recognized the voice of his beloved Ciicothe. Tears flowed from his sightless eyes.

The reunion with her old uncle was beyond any great dream she could have had. Uncle Yellow Robe told of his travel to the south to find a tomb location that overlooked the sacred Ohio River. Their mission was to hide the bones of the Great War Chief Tecumseh from the white scavengers. The remainder of his group was hanged. Without the courageous efforts of Brother Hiram who saved him from the rope, he would surely be in the tomb with the dead.

Thomas described the battle on the Thames where the soldiers killed Tecumseh. He described the valor of Ciicothe's brother, Little Hawk. He could not be sure whether he died on the battlefield or survived, for many members of the tribe were scattered to the four winds.

Willow's stories were heartbreaking for Uncle Yellow Robe and hard for him to endure. She described Tall Walker Woman's last moments on this side of life, her prayers to the man Jesus, and her will to fight to the end. All this made Uncle Yellow Robe proud of this strong-willed woman.

Uncle Yellow Robe and Ciicothe laughed at the white man's name changes that they were forced to make. He explained that the name Thomas was given to him by the Moravian Christian Missionaries at the Gnadenhutten town before the massacre of 1782. As he was now a Christian again, he must use his given name from Christ.

The cabin was a pleasant surprise. Uncle Thomas had kept it remarkably clean, which surprised them due to his blindness. Hiram helped build a loft bedroom for Pete. This space had just enough room for a shuck-filled mattress and storage area for Pete's few belongings.

As promised, Willow was put to work at the David and Sons General Store. Hiram established a small section of apothecaries that supplied native medicines, cures, and remedies, which was of great need in the western region of the United States.

Pete was put to work at David's Landing, one of the busiest ferry ports on the Ohio River east of Cincinnati, operated by Hiram. On the Kentucky side of the Ohio River, at Catlettsburg, Horatio Catlett managed a similar port. Eli Thayer ran the landing in Virginia.

The Ohio port was exceptionally busy, as it received ferries from both Kentucky and Virginia, as well as cargo boats coming from the mouth of the Big Sandy River. For the first time in her life, Willow felt that everything was going to work out for her family.

The months raced by as Willow filled the void for much-needed health care on the Ohio frontier. She had the great fortune to receive continued training from Uncle Thomas (she was finally getting used to his name change, and he, hers). She was learning about new plants, their various uses, and proper mixtures in the ancient stone cup, which she had rescued at North Bend and had successfully used as a weapon in Cincinnati.

Willow was also in demand for her services as a midwife. She had no children herself, nor had she been with a man in the act of sex. However, she quickly gained experience in the skill of childbirth.

Pete had also adjusted to his work. As a dock hand, his strength and growth over the past months were astonishing. He was now the size of a full grown man at sixteen summers old, which may have been due to the hard work at the landing, or the fact that French (his father) was a tall man.

Willow thought that she had seen all the astonishing things about this little community started by Hiram David until this hot, October day when he asked her to follow him to the river landing on the Ohio. When they arrived at the dock, Hiram made a turn up river toward an old, run-down building about three hundred feet from the waterfront. He unlocked the old door, and it squeaked open on its rusty hinges. She was asked to follow him into the darkness.

Hiram struggled to light the oil lamp hanging from the ceiling. Willow's good eye slowly adjusted to the change in light. She saw an opening in the ground lined with oak timbers going straight down out of sight. The air from the pit hit Willow in the face. It had the odor of the ancient Ohio riverbed and was making the sound of a demon sucking wind.

Hiram explained the concept of the Underground Railroad and his connection to the abolitionist movement. He told Willow about his trust in her, and of the great number of slaves he had helped to gain freedom. He described how the tunnels were dug. This tunnel split into two directions, one branch going to Virginia and the other going to Kentucky. He told her about the deaths during the construction of the tunnels and the "Dead or Alive" bounties placed on the heads of the Underground Railroad conductors, who were never safe.

All of this information he shared with Willow to recruit her help as a leader for the Underground Railroad. There was an extreme need for conductors to travel deep into Virginia and help lead the slaves to freedom. At present, most of the conductors had a bounty on their heads. It was becoming too dangerous for some of the volunteers to continue making these trips. Hiram asked her to sleep on her response. Willow knew she did not need a night to think on the subject. The Reverend Rankin had already planted that seed in her heart. She could give an answer here and now, "Yes!"

The slave rescue runs south took place quickly. At first, Willow traveled with the others. After she had learned the routes, she went on her own. She could blend in with most people because her English was excellent. Willow's manner was pleasant, and most people did not notice the burn scars on her face, as she always wore a sunbonnet that also helped keep her complexion light in color.

Three years of the happiest time of Willow and Pete's lives had passed. Their cabin had been expanded to add a private bedroom for Uncle Thomas.

His mood had improved due to the good family treatment and extra food prepared by Willow. Some of the native Indian recipes were a special treat for her old uncle.

Uncle Thomas's health had also improved with Willow's tender care in preparing his medicines. But during the past week, he started telling anyone that would listen that the time for his death was near. He was adamant with Willow that the time had come for him to show her the location of his tomb, the place where the bones of the great Tecumseh rest. This was the place he wanted to be interred with the great Shawnee leader and as his own final resting place.

Old Thomas was close to sixty summers old now. Willow knew his sight was almost gone and most likely could not find the location of this grave. She challenged him on this issue. He quickly told her that his vision was not a problem; the sight of his mind's eye was perfect. He could lead her there without leaving the cabin.

Old Thomas began describing the landmarks, the distance from their cabin, and the exact direction. From this precise, detailed information Willow believed she could easily get to the tomb. Willow had followed the route given her by Uncle Thomas. The landmarks were more accurate than she could have prayed for. Old Thomas's mind's eye was clearer than she thought possible. Just ahead was the rock outcropping that looked like a human skull.

Willow found the deer path that cut through a rough thicket of saw-toothed briers. She inched her way into the thicket, tearing her dress in her attempt to get to the rock face. At this point, Willow knew she must change clothes and bring the tools she needed to access this tomb. She would need to return the next day.

As Willow exited the brier patch, a booming voice called to her. "What the hell are you doing on my property, you Indian scum?" came the sound of a man's voice. Willow looked to see an old, scrawny, white man holding a Kentucky long gun pointed at her head. She knew from his trembling hands that the gun could go off at any time. She had to think quickly.

Willow explained that she was searching for the Indian herbs used for making the medicines for sale at David and Sons General Store. The old man immediately lowered the rifle and apologized, as he recalled how her remedy saved his wife from certain death last winter.

The man gave Willow permission to hunt the roots on his land anytime she had a need for them. He was appreciative of her medicines and sorry from his heart for his treatment towards her. Indians had killed his son in the battle of the fallen timbers, and the death continued to sour his soul towards her people.

The incident at the skull rock tomb had a profound effect on Willow's attitude. She now believed that she must own and protect this sacred land, although she had no concept of individual ownership of land. This was a foreign concept to the beliefs of the Indian people and their way of life. She would approach Hiram for help.

Willow knew from stories told to her by Uncle Thomas that if they had not moved the bones of Tecumseh to the Ohio tomb, the white man would never have stopped until they had desecrated his grave in Canada. The white man had no respect for the Indian ancestor's bones. They had desecrated Indian graves for three hundred years. Uncle Thomas described the work of the Canadian farmers trying to bury the fallen warriors on the battlefield at the Thames. The American soldiers worked ahead of the farmers by scalping and cutting body parts off some of the warriors while they were still alive.

The soldiers fought over one corpse with particular joy, as they thought it was the body of Tecumseh. One excited soldier removed the scrotum bag from this body for use as a coin purse while another cut off the fingers. Willow immediately knew the importance of her solemn duty of protecting the tomb of Tecumseh.

Willow was pleased with the quick response by Hiram. He had offered help with money and any legal matter needed to acquire this property. She showed him the bank notes and the gold that she had taken from the North Bend mansion.

After counting the sum, Hiram looked at Willow in total shock. There were over four thousand dollars in United States bank notes, not counting the value of the gold coins! It was little wonder the general wanted her caught, and his property returned. Had Hiram taken the time to read the general's letters that Willow had in her possession, he would have realized the great value of that packet as well. And the real danger they were all in.

Hiram handled the realty transfer without any problems. Had the local land authority known Willow was a full-blooded Indian, she could not have owned this acreage. Construction began the same year on Willow's new home. It sat on over six hundred acres of rich, Ohio, river bottom land with good, spring fed water to supply all of their needs.

The front porch would have a panoramic view of the beautiful, Ohio, river bottom, with the rear porch facing towards the hills. The sacred tomb of Tecumseh was in the distance. The remaining acreage to the northeast was hilly and covered with old growth timber of oaks, poplar, willow, and the great buckeye. The old river road passed through the south portion of this property near the banks of the Ohio, which allowed safe transportation of their needs.

The general's money was, at last, some value to Willow. She would use the remainder of the fortune to pay for the furnishings of this big house. She would also build a storage shed for her supply of medicines to help the people of this area.

Willow lived up to her commitment to Uncle Thomas and visited the rock tomb on numerous occasions throughout that year. The urgency in her old uncle's voice, each day crying the death songs of the ancestors, confirmed the need for action. Willow learned that the reason for the selection of this burial site by the ancient people was obviously due to the difficulty of gaining access from any side. She suffered injuries each time she visited this place, yet found great peace in her heart when she sat on this massive, flat-top stone and prayed for guidance from God.

The year of 1829 started out with great sorrow for Willow and her family. Old Thomas died after several years of predicting his life was about to end. Willow completed the burial ceremony in secret, with only Hiram, his two sons, and Pete in attendance.

With many difficulties, the remains of Thomas were taken in secret by

Willow and Pete to the burial chamber cave; the final resting place of the Great War Chief Tecumseh. It took three hours to cut through the brier patch to make an accessible path. When they arrived at the base of the stone, the climb was straight up with a turnout ledge on the top rim.

There were hand and foothold cutouts spaced evenly in the face of the massive rock carved by some ancient tribe more than a thousand summers ago. The cutouts into the stone face were most likely made for the same type of burial. Willow and Pete now had to make this same sad journey.

Pete was a tall, strong man of twenty summers old. Now, his strength would be tested. The hemp rope with boat hoist rigging from Hiram's general store was invaluable. To attach this rigging to a huge oak tree that grew next to the skull stone was the only way they could have accomplished the task of getting the body to the top. The rigging came loose and almost pulled Pete to his death. His strength allowed him to recover, which stopped the free fall of old Thomas. The opening at the top was as small as a chimney. With oak limbs used to support the rigging, they lowered old Thomas head first into the tomb entrance.

The body was placed east to west as was the Shawnee custom. They lined the body with the bark of the buckeye and willow trees. These trees provided great healing powers for his next life. There were offerings of kinnikinnick smoking mixture, his stone pipe, and other personal belongings. Willow was shocked not to see the Jesus cross around his neck.

Willow paused to look around. She was surprised at the size of the burial chamber. The light of the safety lantern blazed to life showing the primitive signs etched into the soft stone. The unfamiliar writing on the walls was carved adjacent to some graves where even the bones had decomposed and turned to dust.

The opening was tiny in comparison to the space under the massive rock. The grave platform that she believed was Tecumseh's was relatively new compared to the other graves. There was an odd, screaming look of pain on the skeleton of this decomposed body.

They finished with a solemn Christian prayer for Thomas, and a Shawnee prayer for both him and Tecumseh. Willow removed the Masonic medallion from around her neck, which was given to her by Hiram so many summers ago near the banks of the Tippecanoe River. She topped old Thomas's head with this emblem to show her great love for this man, and then laid his most beloved possession in his hand, his dog-eared Bible.

The journey home was difficult knowing Uncle Yellow Robe was in the tomb. Willow knew he would not be there to bring comfort to her in the trying times to come. She took great solace in knowing Uncle Yellow Robe was with her beloved mother, Tall Walker Woman. And with the Great Good Spirit's will, she would someday join them.

The other grievous event of 1829 was worse than old Uncle Yellow Robe's journey to the Grand Master of the Universe. The white devil (Wahcanaquah Matchamanetto), Andrew Jackson, won the presidential election and moved into the Great White Father's House in Washington. The white men called him King Andrew, the Indians called him the devil or evil spirit. He was the man who said, "The only good Indian is a dead Indian." He lived up to that statement during his term as president by killing the Indian men, women, and children.

CHAPTER 9

Tecumseh's Curse   1830-1834   on the Ohio

The white devil Jackson, a man who had killed for as little as an insult, had now settled into the White House. With him, he brought his belief that the only good Indian is a dead Indian. Jackson was moving forward with his illegal Indian Removal Act, intending to force all of the tribes to relocate to the reservations and concentration camps west of the Great River. All of the white man's treaties could then become what they were intended, paper to wipe their behinds.

Willow had settled into her new home. She was working at the general store gaining a good reputation with the citizens of the apothecary trade in southern Ohio. The additional remedies that were taught to her by Uncle Yellow Robe before his death had proved to be vital for this community's health.

Being in high demand as a midwife was very pleasing to Willow's heart, as she loved the birthing of babies. All of the attention and gratitude of the community could, mayhap, lead the old general's evil thugs to her location. Willow had to be on her guard constantly. Southern Ohio had become the center of the abolitionist movement in this country. Willow worked hard to stay within the ghost realm of the underground, thereby keeping her identity concealed. This became more of a challenge each day.

The Reverend Rankin had moved to the forefront of the abolitionist movement with his published letters concerning slavery's sins. Through Hiram David's association with the underground movement, Willow had continued her friendship with this man of faith. She also found new friends within the national abolitionist movement. When the southern states put a reward of five hundred dollars on her head, her new contacts assisted in hiding her identity. They knew that the evil that was lurking in the dust could get the bounty for her life.

At first, Willow and Pete had rested well in their new surroundings. They received a tremendous amount of pleasure from the rear porch view of the skull rock tomb and had a good feeling of security from this sacred place. They felt the Great Good Spirits were watching over them while they guarded this consecrated land.

Within the last six months, Willow began to have dreams. At first, they were pleasant with visions of the green corn ceremonies, the dancers during the great hunting ceremonies, and the happy times before the long knives stole the South Wind people's souls and their way of life. On this cold September night, Willow drifted from a deep sleep to a state that she thought was fully awake. She was a small child again sitting in a full circle of women as a ghostly figure approached her. She and the other children were shucking dried corn to prepare for the long, cold winter to come.

The face of the Great War Chief Tecumseh manifested. The worries and torment that lined his face from the many battles for his people gave him a somewhat stern look. He spoke only to Willow. In the musical language of the Shawnee people, he asked, "Remember the dog, Mad Anthony Wayne, and his fate at the Presque Island?" Then, he held his hands out to her and revealed the blood-soaked buckeyes he was holding. She remembered the legend of Wayne's death at the hands of the Shawnee's revenge, the warrior's buckeye poison.

Willow woke to a loud crashing noise on the hill behind the house. She thought that she had heard the sound in her dream until Pete almost knocked her over to get to the rear door. There was a fire burning the trunk and bare limbs of an old, dead, buckeye tree only a hundred feet from the tomb of Tecumseh.

The next day they found that the same buckeye tree was still smoldering at the base of its massive trunk. The lightning storm that did this damage had passed. This omen, along with the continued dreams and visions, had Willow's nerves very unsettled. She knew these events had great importance.

The following morning workmen were back on the job of building a barn with an attached smokehouse for Willow, as they had completely outgrown the small outbuildings. They were setting stones for the foundation while Pete helped level a heap of soil. Pete stopped and ran to the house. His face was ashen, and he was having trouble getting his words out. Finally, he motioned for Willow to follow him.

When they arrived at the work site, the men were standing in a circle around the mound. Willow saw what had their gape-mouthed attention. In the center of the pile was the skull of a giant. The lower jawbone was large enough to wrap around the head of a normal-sized man.

Willow remembered the stories about the South Wind people's refusal to have permanent towns in the Kentucky land. The ghost people of the lost, giant, white Azgens Tribe continued to walk as ghosts on the trails and river bottoms. They had always caused bad luck for all who lived on their bones.

Suddenly, Willow realized she must move the location of the barn. She would conduct a Shawnee ceremony to rebury these bones back in their original burial mound to respect the people who placed them there a thousand summers ago. Willow found no signs of the burial of any other ancient people in this area.

Willow buried the bones, but the stone tablet with the illegible words remained uncovered while she conducted the Shawnee ceremony. Once she prayed for forgiveness of disturbing the sleep of these ancient people, Willow buried the tablet in its original place with the bones. Her reputation for the conduction of this type of ceremony spread fast, as numerous people were uncovering graves in this area of southern Ohio. Blaming their bad luck on the bones, some people would ask for her help. Others would build on top of the bones anyway, no matter the future price for them or their families.

Poage's Landing, which was on the Kentucky side of the Ohio River, was laced with large, Indian burial mounds. The people there were building their homes, businesses, streets, and churches on top of the bones. They used the sacred earth of these mounds to fill the low wetlands of their town, stealing the artifacts of the graves as they moved the soil. In a few cases, some of the God-loving people of Poage's Landing would ask for Willow's help. Yet in most incidents, they took their chance with fate.

After the reburial of the bones and artifacts of the ancient, giant people, Willow's dreams returned to cheerful events of her childhood and the joyous ceremonies of the South Wind people. Willow identified seven mounds in a circle from the cave tomb where the bones of Tecumseh rested. She recited the Shawnee and Christian burial prayers at each site and placed a stone marker on the top of each mound; having done this, she hoped the spirits would rest in peace.

The evil Jackson had now resided in the White House for three years. This devil had pushed his illegal Indian Removal Act into law. This act added misery for the Indian tribes remaining in Ohio. The pressure to relocate these people was growing.

The Treaty of Greenville had promised the tribes land in northwest Ohio for as long as the forests grew and the waters ran. The fine print did not guarantee that the white man would not cut down all of the trees. Nor did it promise that the white man would not stop the flow of the rivers with dams, kill the animals or poison Mother Earth. If they accomplished any of these things, they would be disregarding this same treaty.

Willow had seen the devastation done to southern Ohio. Everywhere she went she saw the remnants of digging for iron ore, coal, and limestone used to make a small amount of iron. The iron furnace used to produce this iron was constructed of large blocks of stones quarried in the hills, which left gaping holes in the heart of Mother Earth.

White man cut the virgin, native trees (some being five hundred summers old) to feed the hunger of these monsters. The iron was produced to make more weapons that the rich, white man needed to supply the poor people so they could kill other poor people. With the poor killing the poor, it allowed the rich to live in peace and enjoy the fruits of the poor people's labor.

The black man of Ohio fared little better than the Indians. When established in 1803, the state had outlawed slavery. A black person had to prove, in a court of law, that they were not a slave to get a certificate of freedom. If a black man had no certificate, he could not get a job. The sheriff could arrest them and return the black slaves for a reward. These laws also made it very dangerous for anyone harboring a black or working for the Underground Railroad.

Willow knew about these regulations, so when her home was erected she had a root storage cellar built under the house. The cellar was ordinary when first constructed, mayhap to save her from jail or a hangman's rope. There was a secret room added later to hide the runaway slaves.

The trip to Kentucky would be Willow's last for this season. She and Pete had traveled west to the town of Ripley. There they enjoyed the company of the Reverend Rankin at his new home that overlooked the town. The visit confirmed Willow's belief in the work of this brave, good, white man. Sometimes, she was ashamed of her feeble attempts to help this great cause.

Willow and Pete crossed the Ohio River on the ferry at Maysville and traveled east on the Kentucky side of the Ohio River with two slaves. Their goal was to get to the tunnel at Catlettsburg and have a safe crossing into Ohio. The trip went well. They arrived at the Catlettsburg Landing in the morning before the first ferryboat run from the Ohio side.

Pete and Willow entered the shack that concealed the tunnel access. Horatio Catlett helped with the safety lights. The pumps had been running so the entrance was dry. They passed the halfway point when the earth started to rumble. Pete led the group while Willow brought up the rear. The roof began to collapse in behind her. She screamed for them to run, although it was difficult having to run humped over.

The water of the river bottom started to pour in. Willow fell to the floor of the tunnel. Looking up, she saw the light coming from the Ohio side exit. Her three companions scrambled up the exit ladder. Willow got to her feet as the water came rushing around her, pushing her violently towards the Ohio side. Her head hit the tunnel roof's oaken beams.

Willow's mind went black. There was a figure at the Ohio side exit. It was Tecumseh holding out his hand. His grip was firm. While reassuring her, he pulled her from the tunnel into the opening, allowing her to float up.

Willow regained consciousness on the dirt floor of the tunnel shack. She spat up water with traces of blood. Also, some blood began to flow down her face from a small scalp wound. Pete stood over her crying with joy that they had all made it out alive.

The earth had quaked on the Kentucky side, crumbling the roof of the slave tunnel. The earthquake was Tecumseh's curse. But the great chief did not want this to be a grave for Willow (Ciicothe) Reed; she had miles to go and good deeds to complete. This near-death event had more of a profound effect on Willow's present life than she would know. The message that the Great Chief Tecumseh was trying to send her was unclear. He had saved her life for some greater purpose.

CHAPTER 10

The Lost Cherokee   1835-1838   on the Ohio

Willow's months of slow, painful rehab (from her near drowning experience during the slave tunnel collapse) seemed endless. She saw the fall and winter seasons come to an end, wondering many times if she would survive. She spent her nights dreaming about the Great Chief Tecumseh saving her life. The spring allowed her to get out of the house for the first time in three months.

Without the help of Pete and his fiancée Genevieve, Willow knew she would not have survived. They had delayed their wedding to allow her time to recover. Because she was on her death bed, they had feared that on many of the cold winter nights she would die. They almost gave up all hope thinking she would be dead in the tomb with Tecumseh's bones. Prayer to God was their only solace.

The sun felt good on Willow's skin. The weather had changed from rain to an unusual warmth for the month of April in this area of southern Ohio. She was sitting in her cane porch chair daydreaming about the upcoming summer wedding of Pete and Gen. She wondered if Morning Star was smiling in heaven because of these beautiful thoughts. She saw a red hawk soaring high on the billowy clouds. This was a good sign.

In the distance, the sound of a buckboard wagon coming towards the house at a breakneck speed ripped Willow from her pleasant thoughts. The buggy came to a full stop. Pete was at the reigns with blood on his hands.

Near panic, Willow hobbled towards the side of the wagon only to see a man, or what remained of him, lying on a blood-soaked buckboard tarp. His left hand was missing; blood was coming out of his mouth. She was sad for this wretch but relieved that it was not Pete's blood. Willow called for help from the David brothers, Ike and Joe. The brothers stopped their work at her barn and helped her move the severely injured man into her house.

Willow would do everything within her power to save the stranger's life. His unconsciousness was a blessing with all the severe pain he must be enduring. She did her best to save this broken man. The bleeding was under control, and a poultice of pain relieving antiseptic was applied to the stump where his hand once lived.

Willow went to her rear door to talk with the Wilson brothers. They were quarry workers that had arrived in a slow moving oxcart. A mangy dog greeted her with a snarl; she greeted it with the working end of her straw broom. The dog retreated out of harm's way with the orange-colored fur on his back standing erect. He did not take his eyes off the rear door.

The workers explained that the three men were working a stone quarry cutting large blocks of stone for the Hecla Furnace. A loosened stone crushed Eli's arm and leg. They had removed the stone and loaded him into the David's horse-drawn wagon. Luck was with them that Pete was delivering supplies at the worksite or else old Injun Eli would be going to the boneyard, as they admitted their old oxcart was very slow.

Before they departed, the workers wanted to know if Eli would make it. "Only with the Master of the Universe's intervention can this man survive to live another day," Willow answered. The men got in the oxcart and gave her a blood-soaked rag. She opened it to find the injured man's crushed hand.

Willow learned from Pete that this man's name was Elijah Takatoka Dials, a half-breed Cherokee on the run from the mountains of Georgia with his dog Copper. The illegal Indian Removal Act had set him on his journey. He had been working the quarry, cutting stones for the building of the pig iron furnaces that dotted the southern Ohio countryside. She had learned a little more about this man's past.

Eli regained consciousness the next day. Willow had saved his leg for the time being. The bleeding was under control; only time could tell if he would ever walk again. Eli's hand was gone just above his wrist. She put the remains in a box. She did all she could to save as much of his arm as possible. Now, only time and prayers could save his life. Eli's faithful dog, Copper, did not stray far from the rear dooryard while awaiting his master's recovery.

Through her intense work with Eli, Willow had begun to ignore her continuing, deep, lung pain. Her only efforts were to save the life of this man, who she now believed was someone special in her life. Eli relived his journey from North Georgia (part of the Cherokee Nation) during the long months of healing at the home of Willow Reed. The white man's laws of the devil Jackson were forcing all of Eli's people from their homeland.

Eli had traveled for endless days with old Copper on the ancient warrior's path through Virginia and Kentucky arriving in the Ohio country sometime during 1831. He was looking for his Shawnee brothers after learning of their removal from their southern Ohio homelands. This was long before the eradication of the Cherokee.

Eli described how the Cherokee people had adapted to the white man's lifestyle with the wild game being depleted. The Cherokee people began more productive farming and added more domesticated livestock. The white man saw this as a threat to their agricultural business. New laws were passed to prevent the tribes from competing in the farm market.

The final straw for the Cherokee people was the finding of gold! The white man's greed became too powerful for the Cherokee people to overcome. Some Cherokee remained in the high mountains hiding, but only time could tell if they would survive the white man's greed for their land.

Having been promised exceptional land, Eli's brothers and their families were forced to move south. When he learned about the deaths of some of his family on the trail south, his decision to go north into Shawnee territory was made easy. Finding that the Shawnee people were now far north, he went to work cutting the stone needed to construct the white man's iron devil furnace. Eli had decided to become a ghost walker among the white eyes.

Willow's medicines cured the mange on Eli's dog. As his fur grew back, it was an odd, reddish-brown color. She could see where he got the name Copper. The dog, like Eli Dials, had gained considerable weight. Having short legs, Copper's belly dragged the ground erasing his tracks, a useful trick for an Indian dog.

The help Eli provided throughout his recovery by gathering the needed medicine plants was a tremendous asset to Willow's business. Pete was unable to help her after his summer wedding. He was busy working around the clock putting the final touches on his and Gen's new home located on the ten acres Willow gave them as a wedding gift.

Willow had prayed for Eli to stay. She told him about her great need for his help in the apothecary shop. With each year came more customers, and the medicine plants became more and more difficult to find due to the white man's greed of the forest. Eli could use more time to heal, but all he could think about was his unfinished work at the rock quarry.

Eli was on a mission to find and kill the workers who had caused him to be crushed by the massive stone. He did not want to tell Willow about this. Eli had not told her the real story about the rock quarry accident; the key word being "accident."

On that ill-fated day, the Wilson brothers had arrived late for their shift at the quarry. This caused a delay in the cutting of the face stone of the rock overhang. The brothers, as usual, were still drunk from the rotgut, Deer Creek whiskey they had been drinking all night. The rock boss went to David's General Store to buy supplies, leaving Eli to tend to the oxcart.

The brothers had approached Eli. He could see they were drunk and looking for a fight. Before Eli could pull his knife, he was hit from behind with a cut timber, knocking him out cold. The next thing he could remember was his broken body being loaded into the David's wagon by his quarry boss and Pete; his hand was crushed. The lights of his mind went out for weeks until he saw his saving light in Willow's eyes.

Willow's heart broke when Eli departed. He had taken his few belongings and limped down the dusty road. She prayed for his safety. She knew he would have a problem finding work with one hand missing and a leg that barely functioned.

Eli arrived at the quarry. The boss was overjoyed to see that he had recovered. Eli learned that the Wilson brothers had quit this quarry job to work at the Suwannee Iron Works in Lyon County, Kentucky. He was disappointed; the fire of revenge was burning hot in his gut.

Willow worked hard throughout the following year to develop the native medicine trade. She reunited with her friend William Merrell through her contacts in the apothecary business that were buying drugs and selling native herbs for William's developing business in Cincinnati. She knew she was taking a big risk by renewing this friendship. The chance of her location being discovered by Harrison's thugs would increase. But this was a danger she was willing to take after seeing the good that her medicines could accomplish for the poor people of this area.

The people respected Willow for her work. The ones that could pay did, although most of what she received was in trade (a chicken, young hog, or farm produce). Willow always had a surplus of supplies. When the poor people needed food or help, they knew Willow's door was always open.

The past two summers had been rough. The country had fallen into an economic depression. People who had easily found work in the past now had to peck with the chickens. Most folks who had gotten loans to buy land (hoping the value would go up) lost everything. The country was overrun with down-and-out, hungry men without jobs who had their women and children in tow.

The policies of Andrew Jackson and the wild spirit of gambling on land speculation across the country were a lot to blame. The removal of the Indians and the theft of their lands made this possible. But the hell produced from this devil's work was coming down on the current president, Martin Van Buren, and the unlikely event of him gaining a second term loomed largely. He was a hapless pawn in this political game.

The Whig party now controlled the Ohio State House. The Whig Governor Joseph Vance, along with his political party's muscle, was pushing and pulling for the great, war hero of Tippecanoe to run for president. Harrison had failures on the political stage in the past few years. However, having resurrected in a new party, he believed his chances were good.

Homeless camps dotted Willow's land. The people in the camps shared in the work of the farm and harvest. No one would be turned away. The children called her Mama Willow. She helped birth many of these youngsters while performing her midwife duties.

Hiram David's general store and ferry business continued to be a great success. He contributed to the poor people. And always extended a cable tow for the aid of a brother Mason. Hiram's sons, Joseph and Isaac, had been raised in the Masonic Lodge in Kentucky along with Pete, who now looked to his Masonic Brothers as blood brothers and his extended family.

Willow worked to protect the Indian burial mounds and the sacred burial cave of Tecumseh. She allowed the impenetrable brier patch to grow out of control. The brier's thorns were the best natural protection of this secret place. She would not permit the cutting of the virgin timber in the hills to the back of her land, which allowed the forest floor herbs to grow and prosper.

The white man's root hunting technique was to take all the plants' roots. This method satisfied their momentary greed, but they did not think about their future needs. By doing this, they drove the medicine plants close to extinction.

Willow only harvested a small amount of the root stock from each plant. This gave the plants time to recover. She felt responsible for the care and welfare of the poor people camping on her land. She was prepared with a good harvest for a long, hungry moon winter.

CHAPTER 11

Dripping Beaver at the Cold Wave   July 1963   Ironton on the Ohio

I thought I would have a heat stroke on this super-hot, summer day. I had sweat starting in my butt crack, dripping off my nut sack, and leaking to the ground from my short pant leg openings. As if I needed something to turn up the heat, I would soon find it at the next house on my route delivering the *Grit* newspaper; it would be a blowtorch to my balls.

The delivery was routine. The lady of the house answered the doorbell, her robe neatly tied at the waist. She quickly took her *Grit* newspaper and went to get my money. I felt like she was taking a long time. When she returned, I could see what had taken her so long. The robe was untied and fully open giving this immature thirteen-year-old an eye level view of the mature glory bush!

Now I had experienced the joy of the young, bald beaver a time or two, but this baby was full grown! I think she was making it wink at me; I couldn't look away. Baby oil covered her body with sweat dripping down to that hazel-colored pelt. Droplets of that viscous liquid splashed on the door sill. As she placed the money into my trembling hand, I realized I had not looked at her face. When I looked up, she was smiling, slowly pulling her robe together.

I was startled back to reality by the postman coming up the walkway behind me. Maybe all this body lubrication was for him. My beaver watching day was over. I ran down the street only imagining what the postman was doing with the dripping beaver.

Wow! That could be my Indian name, Dripping Beaver. I sure know what I need now. No, it's not what you're thinking. I need a large bottle of good old Cold Wave soda pop. Before I go to Third Street and get juiced up on some Cold Wave soda pop, I need to sell my two remaining newspapers.

I made the wrong decision of making a quick run into the Wagoner's Bar and Grill. There was always a drunkard or two in there who would give three times the price for this raggedy newspaper. If they were real plastered, I could get real lucky and make fifty cents. I made my usual quick move and prayed that the bartender didn't see me. As the going was clear, I moved to the right and sold the first ten-cent *Grit* for thirty cents. My last paper sold in a heartbeat for fifty cents.

The barkeeper eyeballed me and was moving to toss me out of his establishment when I saw my old man in a back booth with a friend of his and two barfly women. That wasn't a big surprise on either account. I didn't recognize any of his drunk cohorts. I prayed that he didn't see me. I darted to the door, but it was too late. The bartender had blocked my exit.

The old man was on me like stink on a dog turd. He grabbed my arm, pulled me out of the bar and around the side of the building. He spit a stream of profanities as he booted my ass all the way. He was trying to undo his belt, no doubt planning a good ass-whooping. As I broke free, I dropped some of my *Grit* newspaper money. I didn't look back until I felt safe. When I cleared the corner of Ninth Street, I could see the old man scooping up my coins from the ground.

I burned shoe rubber running towards Beech Wood Park. I circled the park and headed to the sand pit, only to see Magoo kicking a football on Tanks Memorial Stadium field. I will tell you that Magoo couldn't see his pecker in front of his face, but that joker could kick a football a country mile! It didn't take much to convince Magoo to go with me for a Cold Wave soda pop.

I brought Magoo up to speed on the dripping beaver story. Needless to say he was impressed. Bearded spitting clam was Magoo's name for the body part that I had seen. I had to ask if he had ever seen the bearded spitting clam. But before he could answer a chill went through my body.

The sight that sent chills down my spine was my Grandma Lu walking towards the Cold Wave with a paper bag of groceries in her arms. She was looking at the Wilson Athletic baseball glove building. When we walked up she was speaking to the open air; as she called it, talking to the ghost people. Grandma Lu always gave good advice on this subject. "It's good to hear the voices, and it's ok to answer the voices. But don't let them give you the wrong answers."

Grandma Lu told us she worked in that building many years ago. Not making baseball gloves, but rolling cigars at five cents per box of twenty. She used to work for the John Swisher Cigar Company. Now that's about right, an Indian rolling cigars, go figure.

Not much in life surprises me. But when Grandma Lu apologized to Magoo for running him off two months ago when I was on my death bed, shocked me to the bone. She gave Magoo a big hug. As he turned to go, "Take it easy Bearded Spitting Clam," slipped out of my lips. I forgot my old granny was standing beside us.

Magoo quickly replied, "Be cool Dripping Beaver." As I carried Grandma Lu's bag of groceries to her house, I lamely tried to explain my new Indian name without revealing the story of the real dripping beaver, which was now burned into my mind's eye forever.

We arrived at Grandma Lu's house. While we had walked, she told me that my Grandma Wick had been sick for several days but had improved some that morning. Grandma Wick had asked her to fetch me around, as she was desperate to continue the story of Ciicothe's journey.

I relived the incident at the beer joint with Grandma Lu. After it was said and done, I wish I could get it back in the barn, but that jenny was gone. Grandma Lu looked at me with her coal-black, piercing eyes. We had all had our minds burnt blank by her cold, hairy eyeball stare.

Her quick wit churned out one of her classic nuggets of wisdom while chiding me for going into that bar. "Son you are surely not the sharpest kernel of corn in the turd." Enough said, I couldn't argue that point. I knew what she was trying to say.

The old kinnikinnick was boiling in the stone pipe. Grandma Wick was looking all bright-eyed. Before I could sit down, Grandma Lu stated in an ominous voice, "If you let her, she will run your ass crazy looking for that tomb. You're not the first dumb-ass to have your head filled with all this nonsense."

I'm not sure about Grandma Lu's need to warn me of the hills, maybe she likes bossing my life. I have crawled over every inch of those damn Ironton Indian hills. If anyone could find a tomb without losing their mind, it's yours truly.

CHAPTER 12

The Devil's Election   1839-1840   on the Ohio

The winter of 1839 was as bad as Willow had expected and worse. She had opened her home and heart to anyone needing a place to live. The food that Willow had stored was now depleted. The illness during this winter season was pervasive. She had not planned on feeding the large numbers of poor people that ended up living on her farm.

Everyone suffered from sickness as the marginal shelters available to the poor did not protect the people from the cold. Willow converted her house into an infirmary for the most severely ill. She kept a large caldron of boiling water fired in the back dooryard to sanitize clothing and bedding. She had worked tirelessly for months to save these poor, destitute people.

With spring came some hope that the last of the winter illness was gone. Willow cleared the last of the sickest people from her house. There were only three of the blue hairs that had died and one young girl named Poppy with whom she had grown very fond. She was sad at her inability to save this precious child, believing in her heart that the Master of the Universe had a greater mission for little Poppy.

The planting season had arrived, and with it, the hope of renewed life was in the air. With the help of a group of poor people camping on her land, Willow had gone to the forested hillside to search for the tender sprouts of the spring plants to make the Shawnee elixir. She knew this spring elixir, along with the improved weather, would help the health (if not the spirits) of all the community that consumed her magic greens.

Willow was at the clothing scrub board working the wash in the back dooryard. Copper dog, who had been abandoned by Eli, started barking. He was acting crazy as if he had a bloated tick on his nut sack. The vision in her good eye came into focus; it was her lost Cherokee, Elijah Takatoka Dials! Copper ran full speed to greet his master. The dust on the road boiled up behind him where his pecker drug the ground like the moldboard of a plow.

Eli was there; the years on the road had taken a toll on him. He looked like a walking skeleton of a man. He was so emaciated that Copper knocked him off his feet, licking his face as he lay on the ground unable to get up or move. His eyes were sunken in, and his britches were dropping off his boney ass. Willow thought she was looking at someone as close to death as they could get without being in the tomb. Her heart was broken to see him in this condition.

The months passed quickly, and Eli was making a slow recovery with Willow's help. He regained his weight, giving him the appearance of a young man of thirty-five again instead of an old man of eighty. Eli was working to close out the harvest, collecting as many medicine plants for the upcoming winter as he could, demonstrating his worth to Willow's apothecary trade.

The poor people camping on Willow's land had moved on as the opportunities for work in the area had improved. The lumber and iron industries had taken an adverse toll on the old growth forest. Willow was determined not to allow this to happen to her land.

Willow, Eli and Copper were always together. When you saw one the others were not far behind; they were inseparable. Everyone would joke that they were in love, which was closer to the truth than they knew. Although Willow was now beyond forty summers old (five years older than Eli) her appearance was that of a twenty-year-old girl. She had never been with a man sexually.

On this warm, late October evening, Willow and Eli were sitting on the back porch of her home looking into a full harvest moon. Eli opened up with full honesty, and told her about his hell-bent revenge trip to Kentucky in search of the Wilson brothers, who had attempted to kill him. With intent to kill, they had rolled the stone that almost crushed him at the quarry.

Eli had located the Wilson brothers in a remote town in Kentucky. He quickly killed the first brother, then tracked the other brother for several days in the thick Kentucky woods. He found him in his campsite bed and cut off his head. Eli lived in the woods for two months before being captured and put in jail. He was going to be hanged, if not for the murders of the Wilson brothers, for being of Indian blood.

Eli suffered in jail. He knew the jailer was trying to starve him to death before he could face the hangman (an effort to save a good rope). One way or another, Eli knew he was a dead man if he did not escape. He got his chance just after Christmas when they eased up on security at the jail. Along with two black men, he ran following the slave underground, which helped to protect him from recapture.

Eli told Willow that he knew they were still looking for him and that if she wanted him to go, he would. She looked at him in surprise. Willow did not want him to go, she knew Harrison's thugs were still looking for her as well. She looked at him and said, "We are two lost and broken people, I don't think we need to run anymore." They hugged and started to laugh.

The sunrise that morning was like the first in Willow's life. She and Eli had made love most of the night. They woke in each other's arms, breathing the same air, feeling each other's heartbeat. Willow had found the love of her life in this broken, lost, half-breed Cherokee. She now felt complete in her life, where before she had lost so much.

The weeks passed into the early winter. Willow was happy living with Eli. She now had great news! She was with child, maybe one month along into her pregnancy. When Eli learned of this news, Willow thought he would fly away from his joy. He thought no person could stop him from smiling. The people of the area that Willow had helped for many years were as happy for them as if they were family.

The December snow started early that morning. Before the snow could accumulate, Eli left for work at the David and Sons General Store. Hiram, his two sons, and Pete traveled to Kentucky for the Mason's special dispensation of the degree of Master Mason. At least, that was the reason given for this trip to Frankfort, Kentucky.

Willow knew that in the past, most of the Masons did their work in the warmer months. But she had listened to the conversations around the pickle barrels at the David and Sons General Store and knew this trip involved the next presidential election. Whig Governor Joseph Vance, who was leading the drive for William Harrison (the old general, hero of the massacre of Tippecanoe) for president, controlled the Ohio State House.

Harrison was also running a campaign of anti-Masonic sentiment, which brought the Masons together in Kentucky on this cold, winter day in December 1839. The push to get this evil man in the big, white house had started early in this political season. Playing on the desperation of the numbers of poor people roaming the land with no work or place to hang their hats, it looked to be a sure bet that he would win. Willow did not know what hell and misery the election of Harrison as president held for the Indian people. She knew one thing for sure from Harrison's letters taken from North Bend; it would not be good.

Willow went out to the back dooryard where she had her fire pit burning hot. The big caldron of water was heating for her much-needed warm bath. She could see the vanishing tracks in the snow made by Eli, and the drag marks made by Copper; that picture brought a smile to a dark day. She stroked her extended belly thinking of Eli's baby growing. It brought a warmth over her that the December chill could not penetrate. She approached the iron pot and dipped the wooden bucket into the hot water. Her thoughts were only of her love for Eli and the blessing of their baby to come in the summer.

The fist coming out of the blinding snow connected to Willow's chin on her blind side. Delivered with it was a viciousness intended to kill. The wooden bucket of hot water went flying into the air as she went down in a pool of gray.

Willow came to full consciousness tied to her porch chair next to the fire pit. All of her clothes had been removed. To her horror, when her vision focused, she saw old one-ear Moss. With him was one of the general's thugs with a handgun pointed at her head.

All the warmth she had felt was gone. Her feet and hands were numb, and her core temperature was fading fast. Old one-ear moved closer. With his rancid breath blowing hot in her face, he screamed that if she gave him the general's letters he would kill her fast. He placed the point of his knife into her belly, bringing a stream of blood down her front.

The letters were the key to Willow avoiding misery. She would give them to Moss, or he would cut her into small pieces and burn each piece in the fire while she watched. He pulled the knife point out of her gut then threw a hard punch to her midsection. Willow lost all her breath. Moss pulled down his britches and started to piss on her.

Willow was thinking about how everything may be lost. Eli was not due back until morning. He had gone to the store to keep the iron stove fires going and to protect the supplies from night thieves. With this thought, a scream welled up in her throat.

The explosion of blood and entrails hit Willow in the face as the lead slug exiting Moss's gut blew past her head, missing her ear by less than an inch. The limp body of old one-ear Moss fell like a cut timber. Eli came out of the snow walking with purpose towards Moss's fellow goon who was trying to get a shot off, just missing Eli.

The thug was trying to reload his gun with shaky hands when Copper bit a mouthful of the wretch's crotch, twisting his stumpy neck from side to side. Eli plunged his knife deep into the thug's guts pulling the blade up through his evil, black heart. Eli pushed his dead body to the ground; Copper continued to make a snack of his manhood.

Eli untied Willow and carried her into the house. As Eli worked to dress her wounds, he could hear old one-ear Moss screaming for mercy because he could not feel his legs. He was praying that someone would finish him off. Eli had severed his spinal column with the shot through the back. He would give this dogshit of a man time to make peace with his maker, God or Devil, so mote it be. Eli's first priority was tending to Willow and her needs. He would get back to old one-ear soon enough. That is, if Copper didn't make a meal of him or if he didn't freeze to death first.

The morning came with an easing of the heavy snowfall. Willow's bleeding from her vagina was slowing, giving Eli some hope of their baby living. Eli went outside, and to his surprise found old one-ear still sucking God's fresh air.

Moss had pulled his upper body next to the fire; his naked lower body was frozen to the ground. Copper was deep into the other man's guts. This dog was a master at tunneling in the earth for rats. Eli could only imagine the horror that old Moss endured while watching his buddy's guts being consumed.

Eli was all business adding wood to the hot embers to get the fire back to blazing hot in the fire pit. He removed the iron pot and tripod hanger. Old one-ear Moss continued to cry for a quick death. Eli said nothing.

The fire was raging when Eli put the last of the severed remains of old one-ear Moss's thug friend into the fire. His faithful dog Copper, covered in blood, had a look of disappointment. Eli positioned Moss so he could have a good view of the burning of his friend's remains. Eli didn't want him to miss any of the show.

Now, it was Moss's turn. Eli used the iron poleaxe to cut off old one-ear's legs. Eli was sure Moss felt no pain as his legs were frozen to the ground. Next, Eli severed Moss's manhood, adding it to the legs already burning in the fire. In a quiet whisper, Eli indicated one-ear's next piss would be in hell.

Moss blacked out. Eli got some hot water from the iron pot and poured it over Moss's face until he awoke. Before Moss could pass out again, Eli lopped off one of his arms, which brought a scream from hell out of Moss's soul. Eli knew the pain was real.

Hearing the screams, Willow rushed to the back door and opened it to the site of the blood-soaked snow. Eli was standing over old one-ear trying to revive the devil or what remained of him. Willow called to Eli, asking him to end this as torture was not in her nature. Eli turned and crushed Moss's skull with the axe then put his remains in the fire. Willow was right to end this, but wrong in thinking it was over. As long as Harrison was alive, this was not the end.

Willow forced herself to carry on with her life after the death of her unborn baby. She went through the basics to live. She cried in private for days until her tears ran dry. Willow knew she must go on, for Eli's sake.

Copper was having a great time eating the remnants of bone. Willow was cleaning the fire pit, wanting to be rid of the ashes of Harrison's thugs, who had been consumed by the fire when she saw a miracle on the ground. Willow found the wooden, handmade cross that she had gotten from her beloved Tall Walker Woman at Prophetstown. It was the same cross that dog Moss had stolen from her at French's house on the Wabash. He had unknowingly returned it. Jesus was still on the cross untouched by the flames; to Willow, this was a good sign.

Winter and spring passed; summer came. It was a time when Eli and Willow should be celebrating the birth of a child into their family. Instead, they were crying at the gravesite of a baby not to be. A child killed in the womb by Harrison's thugs for a packet of letters. It took a monumental strength of will from Willow to stop Eli from going to North Bend with a killing in his heart. His lust for the blood of revenge was not satisfied.

The presidential campaign of 1840 was heating up. "The war hero of Tippecanoe," "the honest farmer of North Bend," "the log cabin and hard cider ticket," were all labels for Harrison. These were only a few of the blatant lies used by Harrison's camp to bolster the illusion of their candidate.

In the other camp, the team of Martin Van Buren and Richard Johnson were quickly named "the black ticket" due to Johnson's association with a colored mistress for years, who had died leaving him to bring up two octoroon daughters. The failures of Van Buren's economy (numerous poor people busted and out of work), plus the color issue made things look good for the Whig candidate Harrison.

Hiram David and his sons (Joe and Ike) gathered with Willow, Eli, and Pete on this Election Day in 1840. The results would be unknown for several days. The feeling was that Harrison would surely win. His political camp continued a shameless campaign of the common, log cabin farmer Harrison battling against the wealthy Van Buren, who ate his meals on silver plates with gold forks in a white palace.

Willow knew that having the general's letters was a card she could play. However, the danger to her family may not be worth the reward. The conversation on this day was about the anti-Mason/anti-Indian beliefs that this evil man had. Harrison, with this philosophy totally ingrained in his soul, was one step away from the White House. Eli listened with interest as the blood boiled in his body for revenge. He knew that the Indian people and their families could never have peace if they did not stop this evil man.

Hiram described his plan to go to Washington for the Inaugural in the event that Harrison was elected president. Hiram believed that he could get a better understanding of what type of leader this man would become. Eli heard all of the dribble he could take and stormed out of the store with only one thought in mind: *How am I going to kill this evil bastard, whether he is elected president or not?*

CHAPTER 13

Finding Tecumseh   August 1963   South Point on the Ohio

You might think at this point in this wild story that I am one gullible, little dumb-ass. With what happens next, your beliefs will be justified. Grandma Lu gave her best argument to warn me. She explained in detail how her son Bubby, during the summer of 1934, could have been working for the Civil Conservation Corps at Wayne National Forest.

Uncle Bubby could have helped with the construction at Vesuvius Lake Recreation Area earning a few desperately needed dollars to help support his family during the Great Depression. But, hell no! Instead, he was combing the Ohio countryside, searching the hills high and low, looking for the tomb of Tecumseh; the curse was on him. Now it was my cross to carry. *Lookout hills of southern Ohio, here I come!*

Yes, Grandma Lu also blames all of the US Highway 52 traffic accidents, World War II and the death of my Uncle Bubby on the curse of Tecumseh's tomb. She pointed an accusing, shaky finger at Grandma Wick with her long-stemmed, stone, Indian pipe fueled and fired with the curl of kinnikinnick smoke circling around her head.

Grandma Lu went to her bedroom on a mission, returning with a Swisher Cigar box. She opened the box slowly with great reverence. Then, she cautiously removed a medallion on a deteriorated old leather rope, holding it as if it was a poisonous snake.

I was hesitant but held the necklace in my hands. For just a second, I got a feeling of electric shock, and my hands started to tremble. Looking closely, I could see it was inscribed with a compass topping a square frame, in the center was a large G. I had never seen anything like this emblem before.

To the best of her ability, Grandma Lu explained the Masonic influence on our family and how the Brotherhood has assisted our livelihood in southern Ohio. She also told me about their belief in God "The Architect of the Universe" and how they worked to promote respectable men of true brotherhood.

The box also contained an indistinguishable stone and an Indian smoking pipe with the stem broken in two. As Grandma Lu rolled the bowl around in her hand, she told me it was Tecumseh's pipe that had been used for sixty years by Grandma Reed. I looked in the small cigar box. I was startled and fell backwards, catching myself on the table before I hit the floor. I looked at Grandma Lu. She nodded her head up and down saying, "Bones!"

Grandma Lu told me that the mission my Grandma Wick was putting me on was to return these items to the tomb, thereby lifting the curse from our family, which was the result of grave-robbing by my Great-Great Uncle David. My eyes popped open, and the light bulb in my head came on for the first time. Finally, I realized why my head was being filled with this story. Grandma Lu handed me a black cherry Cold Wave soda pop. She could see that I was visibly shaken and knew my mind must be spinning. I had a thousand questions about the bones that looked like a hand.

After I had gotten over the shock of seeing the hand bones in the cigar box, I asked the question that I thought I already knew the answer to. I was right. The bones were of the severed hand of my great-great-great grandfather, Eli Takatoka Dials!

Now I know my mission. I am to find the tomb and return the items that were removed from it over one hundred years ago. With God's help, it may lift the curse from our family. Then, my Grandma Wick could die in peace. Wow! Nothing to it!

Knowing my dad's warnings about Indians, I was thankful for at least one thing: that this box didn't contain a set of petrified testicles and a penis.

Only joking, I know that would be rotted meat by now. But, you know, my family has kept stranger things in a box.

The weather was decent when Web, an old family friend, dropped me off at South Point. My raggedy bike easily fit in the cave-like trunk of his old Packard Clipper. He slowly pulled away and a cold chill ran the length of my spine. I was on my own. His ride got me beyond the high, rock face on the river road past the big, iron bridge crossing the Ohio River into Ashland, Kentucky.

I passed under the old, single-lane, wooden, mule bridge high above the river road. This bridge led to the entrance of the mine dug in the side of the hill where they extracted the clay used to make the Carlyle Tile. People say the mules are blind from working underground. *Maybe that would be my fate if I get trapped underground in Tecumseh's tomb: a blind dumb-ass.*

I came prepared with a flashlight, extra batteries, rope, a sharp knife, a bologna sandwich, and a Cold Wave pop. Old Dripping Beaver was ready! Now all I needed to do was find the hole in this rock. I had already searched for several weeks in vain. This would be my last hurrah for the summer.

When I found the rock, it was almost as I had envisioned it from the description given to me by Grandma Wick. What was even more amazing was that she had not been to this place in more than seventy-five years. It may have been in 1885 when she was my age, thirteen.

I wormed my way through the brier thicket, and after what seemed like an hour, I got to the rock face and tied off my rucksack. I started to climb the hand and footholds. The free end of my rope tied to my belt loops would allow me to pull my supplies up once I made it to the top. I made good progress getting to the overhang. Without the help of an old buckeye limb overhanging the rock, I would not have gotten there.

Once I got to the top of the monolithic stone, I looked down each side. The drop was about fifty feet to the ground, and there was no jumping down. It sure looked further than fifty feet! My butt was now puckering to the beat of my heart. As I took in this panoramic view of the Ohio River, I was sure of one thing: I was crazy to be doing this!

I could not see an opening to a cave tomb. There was a lot of green moss growing on top of this ancient stone monolith. As I started to remove some of the moss, I saw the carvings in the rock made by people more than a thousand years ago. *It is just as Grandma Wick had described it! The search is over! This is Tecumseh's tomb!*

Daylight was fading. Having already planned to stay the night, I brought a raggedy blanket for a bed, as well as some food and drinks. I had a feeling of security in this place. I felt like no person or thing could get to me. I now understand the euphoric feeling Ciicothe must have had while sitting on top of this tomb.

I ate half of my cold bologna sandwich and washed it down with a Cold Wave pop. For dessert, I had a piece of Grandma Lu's fry bread with blackberry jam. All I could think of while laying on my hard bed (with my ancestors under me and looking into the star-filled, warm, August night sky) was that it don't get any better than this.

While thinking that I must have some of Tecumseh's blood running through my body, I dozed into a sound, dreamless sleep. I was dead to the world for what seemed like hours when an animal screeched on the forest floor as if it was on a fast train to hell. I wet my pants. Then, almost falling off the rock fifty feet to the ground, I struggled to find my knife and flashlight, as if that would help. My euphoric feelings left me.

I figure you're wondering where my Indian blood went. I think I peed it out. Yes, that animal may quickly climb one of the tall trees, jump onto this rock, and eat me. All that would remain of me would be one big pile of animal poop. No one would ever say, "Oh, look! There's some Indian blood in that bear dung." Nope, not going to happen.

The sunrise found me awake with my old blanket around my shoulders. I was clutching my **Eveready,** and gripping my knife as if I were going to challenge a full-grown black bear. I needed to get my focus back on my mission. After eating the last of my fry bread, I started looking for the tomb opening.

Walking to the wider side of the boulder, I found what I was looking for the hard way. I slipped on a layer of moss and ended up catching myself with my outstretched arms, cutting and bruising them all the way up to my armpits. With great effort I pulled myself out of the hole, which cut into my ribs as I wormed my way out.

I laid on the cold rock twisting in pain for what seemed like an hour. I wished my main man Magoo was with me for backup; or at least to laugh me through this mess. At last, I recovered enough to inspect the chimney-sized hole in the flat top of this monolith of sandstone.

Looking down the hole, I could see the bottom about forty feet below. I believed I had a length of rope that could reach the tomb floor. Now all I needed was something to tie off to that would hold my weight. I tossed the rope over a large, oak limb and tied it off. Then, I lowered the other end into the hole.

When I looked down the shaft, I could see that the rope was touching the floor of the tomb. The rope was knotted at intervals to allow for easy climbing. I pulled the rope back up, tied off my rucksack, and lowered it to the floor. I was ready to go in. I said a prayer and started down the rope.

I was surprised at how easy my descent was. Maybe all of the times that I was punished in gym class by climbing the endless ropes was paying off, go figure. I located the flashlight as fast as I could because I was scared of the dark. On top of that, I thought I heard a voice groaning on the other side of the wall. I was about to poop my pants!

I had to lay flat to crawl downward through the opening into the burial chamber, pushing the loose dirt out of my way ahead of me with my rucksack of goodies. When I cleared the opening, I returned to my feet. I was astonished at the size of this cavern!

Wood ornamentation and one hundred fifty-year-old petrified bark covered the bone remains. At the hand of one skeleton was an ancient book. *My sweet Jesus Christ, it's Uncle Yellow Robe's Bible!* I located remains that appeared to be Eli Dials, the missing hand was a dead giveaway.

As I moved closer, I almost dropped my flashlight. On top of the human remains were bones of an animal. I am sure these were the remains of a poor animal that had fallen through the entrance hole. The flashlight started to fade out as I was placing the last few items with their rightful owners. I said a quick prayer for Tecumseh, Eli, Uncle Yellow Robe, and any other ancestors hanging out in here. *Mission complete!*

Not wanting to stay one minute longer than needed, I scrambled through the opening. Then, I remembered that I had forgotten my rucksack. I quickly decided that a knapsack with a couple of empty Cold Wave pop bottles and a half-eaten bologna sandwich could only add to a great archeological find. *I can see the headlines:* **ANCIENT PEOPLE LOVE A GOOD COLD WAVE BLACK CHERRY POP WITH BOLOGNA SANDWICH.** As I finished burying the opening to the tomb, I prayed that leaving my things behind wouldn't put a curse on me.

I rushed to the rope as my flashlight was going dead. My spare batteries were in the tomb. I put the light in my back pocket and quickly started to climb. The fading light was making weird-looking silhouettes on the cave walls. I heard the crack of the oak limb, and I could do nothing as I started to fall backwards.

I hit the ground of the tomb foyer knocking the breath out of me and causing the broken flashlight to shoot out of my back pocket, hitting the stone wall. I thought a bone might have popped out of my back, or a hard turd from my ass. With all the pain I felt, it could have been both. I was out of it for a minute while trying to catch my breath. The only light I had was coming through the chimney hole above my head.

As I continued to try to catch my breath, it felt as if I had broken a rib. When I was able to stand, I was light-headed at first and unable to find the rope. I prayed that my line had caught onto something, or else an archeologist would find one raggedy hillbilly kid along with the other things in this tomb. I tugged on the rope, praying that it would hold; it did. I started to climb to that portal of light. I reached the opening, the limb was straddling the hole.

I maneuvered past the tree limb into the blessed light of day and laid on the stone thanking the good Lord for his help. I covered the hole with a frame of limbs and moss and cleaned up anything that would lead to the opening being discovered. Thinking that I completed this dirty deed and lifted the curse from my family, I headed for Grandma Lu's house.

CHAPTER 14

Eli's Coming   Winter 1840-1841   Cincinnati on the Ohio

Although no invitation had arrived (nor were they expecting one) Willow and Eli took several weeks during January and planned a trip to Washington DC. The looming inauguration of William Henry Harrison was fast approaching. Mayhap, if Willow came with the secret tattered bundle of letters and Harrison's gold dowry as a gift, she would get invited to the White House. But then, she would most likely get a musket ball to the head for her efforts.

Willow worked with every fiber of her body through the Christmas season to keep Eli from making a murderous mission to Cincinnati. He had his sights set on killing Harrison at the cabin in North Bend. Eli's desire was never to see Harrison make the inauguration and certainly not one day as president. Eli was unconcerned with making a useless trip to Washington because he was going to North Bend.

On January 26th, the old general was to depart from the port in Cincinnati to travel to his new home, the White House. Eli, with his murderous thoughts, planned to change that. In his heart he knew there was less of a chance to kill this evil dog in Washington, he must do the deed in Cincinnati.

Eli was poised outside the Henrie House in Cincinnati on January 25, 1841. He was shaking from the cold and sickness that had befallen him on his mission to kill Harrison. The Henrie House was set to receive Harrison as its king, as it is always done in the finest courts in Europe. Eli Dials was set to receive him with a slug of iron to the head. Eli lay in the cut long after midnight, cold to the bone and now getting the grippe. He had missed Harrison's arrival due to the massive crowd of well-wishers pushing to get a closer look at their new president.

The old general emerged from the Henrie House well after midnight; the crowds were gone. Eli leveled his pistol, taking aim at the head of the man who would be king of the world. The hammer fell on wet powder with a dud of a spark. No iron ball came out to bust this evil man's skull; the chance had passed. The general was in his coach; his driver tapped the horse, and the carriage was gone. Eli staggered back to the dump of a hovel, only thinking of getting some rest. Mayhap, he would have another chance in the morning.

Eli awoke on Tuesday, January 26th to the sounds of the hogs he was sharing his hovel with. He needed food, drink, and a long gun if he had any hope of killing this evil man. The crowds would force him to shoot from a long distance. The chance of getting close enough to kill him with a tomahawk was very slim. Eli approached the crowds at the port of Cincinnati. He could see the Ben Franklin Steamboat lashed to the dock. There was a rush of activity on its main deck.

As Eli drew closer with his newly acquired buffalo gun, he could see the old general. It was as if he was a king receiving gifts from the well-wishers. Presents of fine canes, baskets of food, and more were all given to his black slave for safe keeping. Eli knew he could not get close enough for a fair, accurate shot due to the large crowd. From the talk of the townspeople, he learned the Ben Franklin would make a stop at Maysville, Kentucky where he could get a good shot from the Ohio side of the river.

As the old general was finishing his long-winded speech to the lively crowd in Cincinnati, the Ben Franklin Steamboat pushed off from the dock. With a bellow of smoke from the twin stacks, she was headed east on the Ohio. Eli was on horseback on the river road headed east toward Ripley with blood in his eye. He was thankful for the warm January day as he galloped past the throngs of farmers lining the Ohio River to get a look at old Tippecanoe.

While the general was waving to the crowds from the deck of the Ben Franklin, the military companies aboard and on shore exchanged gun salutes while the brass bands played. Eli's thoughts were of the evil layered on his family by this man, and of what he needed to do.

Aboard the Ben Franklin, heading east midstream on the Ohio, Harrison continued to love the attention, pressing the flesh of the Ohio and Kentucky Whig contingent traveling to Washington for the inaugural. Also, in his personal suite was his nephew, granddaughter, and three grandsons.

Harrison's daughter-in-law, Jane Findlay Harrison, would go to the White House as hostess while Mrs. Harrison recovered from an extended illness. From the handrail, the old general looked at his supporters lining the riverbank, all calling out, "Tip-Tip-Tip," waving their hats, handkerchiefs, and hands. He smiled, for mayhap the last time, with extreme satisfaction as he waved his hand.

A steamboat that carried a contingent of federal troops arrived before the Ben Franklin to provide security on the riverbanks and to control the hurrahing crowds. The Ben Franklin docked just as Eli thought it would. And, as he expected, it was to overnight at Maysville, Kentucky.

Eli could see the preparations of large bonfires along the banks of the Kentucky side of the river as he was waiting on the Ohio riverbank southeast across the river from Maysville. His hand was cold and shaky. He was praying for a steady hand (or stump in his case) to take a shot at Harrison as this may be his last chance to kill this evil dog.

Eli took his shot as the old general was shaking hands with the well-wishers from Maysville coming aboard the Ben Franklin. The cover of rifle salutes firing from each shore could not entirely cover the explosive sound of the massive buffalo gun that Eli had shot. The iron slug struck the wooden, upright beam of the steamboat, within inches of the president-elect, causing a shower of splinters to hit the crowd.

The old general quickly moved to the interior of the steamboat. Stumbling behind him were the other dignitaries on board the Ben Franklin, some almost falling off the boat. Eli could see soldiers moving towards his position. He quickly got on his horse and departed for the

Reverend Rankin's home in Ripley where he would find a safe-house and recover from the illness that was making him insane.

Eli had three days of warmth and medicine, which may have saved his life. The good Reverend Rankin, who he had worked with in the various movements of the Underground Railroad, treated him as if he was family. Eli did not tell Reverend Rankin of his murderous mission to kill the president-elect, of which he had failed.

The newspapers raved of the president's overnight stay in Maysville. There was a short line describing the almost tragic, errant slug from the celebratory gunfire, but all was well that ended well. Eli must now return to Willow with the bad news.

CHAPTER 15

Lumpkin's Jail   February 1841   on the Potomac

Eli arrived at South Point with a sad heart after his failed attempt to kill Harrison. To his surprise, Willow had moved forward with arrangements for their transportation to the inaugural in Washington. She made this decision after the Ben Franklin's stop at Ashland, Kentucky.

Willow had been watching the spectacle from the Ohio side of the river. She could see the old general on the steamboat. It appeared as if he were looking directly at her as if he knew she was there. She knew in her heart that this madness would not be over until he rotted in his grave.

Their group would travel by steamboat to Pittsburg. They prayed for no icing on the Monongahela River, as this could prevent them from reaching the Brownsville landing. If icing became a factor, the motley group would rent a carriage to complete the journey east. Pete and the David brothers would also make the trip, each going with a different mission in mind. Eli was not the only person with murder in his heart.

The Ben Franklin, with the President-elect Harrison on board, made stops at Portsmouth on the Scioto, Ashland, Old Poage's Landing in Kentucky, Marietta, and Wheeling before arriving in Pittsburg. The trip from Cincinnati to the Brownsville Landing on the Monongahela River consumed seven days. In Brownsville, Harrison boarded a shiny, new coach decorated with scenes from the old general's life, including the massacre at Tippecanoe.

Willow and her party arrived in Pittsburg on a bitter cold, February night. As they expected, the Monongahela River was iced over. The

Masonic safe-house provided for them by Hiram David was warm, and it had a covered shelter for the horses. They had only three weeks to arrive in Washington before the inauguration of William Henry Harrison, which was to be held on the fourth day of March. And with it, he would bring his changes for this country that could never be corrected in a thousand moons.

The Cumberland Road was frozen and as rough as a clothing washboard. The mountains throughout the gap at Cumberland were rugged and covered with snow. The wagon slipped off the road numerous times. The left front wheel had two broken wooden spokes. They were holding on to their hopes and prayers. Only if God was with them would they make it to the safe-house in Virginia. That would put them close enough to the Chesapeake and Ohio Canal where a flatboat could take them on the canal southeast to the falls of the Potomac.

Willow waited in the wagon with Eli. Pete and the David brothers went in to arrange for lodging at McIlhenny's Tavern and Inn in Hagerstown. The condition of the wagon would not allow them to continue on to the safe-house twenty miles south of the Cumberland Road in Virginia.

Pete and the David brothers returned quickly as they knew it was bitter cold for the others who were waiting. The lodging was small but warm. The brothers learned that the old general had stopped at this same inn only two weeks before. Willow knew they needed a break in the weather if they were to make the inauguration on the fourth of March.

For the first time, Willow told the group about the contents of the letters she had taken from the old general's mansion at North Bend, and of Harrison's belief that the slavery issue was one of his most important missions in politics. Harrison would do everything within his power as president to keep slavery, even if it required the split of this nation.

Harrison's Whig Party backers from the south wanted a strong slaver in the White House. The slave states now had what they needed. They knew of Harrison's secret plans for southern slave states to secede from the union if need be. He would soon take the presidency, and they must stop him.

Pete and the David brothers convinced Willow that they could expose this information, ruining Harrison's plans, and the Free states' outcry opposing slavery. Then, the southern death grip on their slaves could be broken. Eli had other plans for this president. He had dreamed of ways to kill this evil man. He truly wanted him to suffer a slow, painful death, and then a quick slide into hell.

They awoke refreshed to find the morning with heavy snowfall and the prospect of their broken wagon. The trip further east would either be delayed or end here in Hagerstown. They breakfasted, then went to the livery to check the status of the wagon. Willow was overjoyed to see its return. They could now continue southeast to the Masonic safe-house and their connections on the Potomac.

The snow had increased as they progressed south. The crossing of the iced-over Potomac went well. With the blinding snow, they all believed that they were lost in the Virginia Mountains. Willow was the first to hear the faint, mournful song coming from over the next rise. She looked at the others for an answer; no one had a response.

As the group of weary travelers crested the rise, they could see a huge campfire and the smell of meat cooking. They stopped while Ike took out his looking glass to get a better survey of the camp before they rode in. The site that greeted him was not good.

There were five black slaves chained together near the fire's heat radius. Tending the fire and cooking the meat was an ancient black man. One white man was there guarding them all with his handgun. A second white man was pulling a young, black girl towards the covered wagon just outside the fire clearing. The girl, mayhap ten years of age, was fighting for her life. Her clothing was partially ripped off, and she had blood coming from her mouth.

Their plan was simple. The David brothers would confront the guard at the campfire with their guns. Eli and Pete would take care of the action in the slavers' wagon while Willow controlled their own wagon outside of danger's reach.

Nothing was going as planned. The guard was startled as he looked up into two guns. He leveled his weapon ignoring Ike's command to drop it. He fired without flinching and hit Joe in the shoulder causing him to drop his gun. Ike's slug went true, directly between the slaver's eyeballs. He fell, dead on the spot.

The action in the wagon began with Eli entering the back flap with his knife in his good hand. His stump was covered with the leather from his old medicine bag. A river-rounded, clear stone (his pawawka, found when he was a child in the cold mountain waters of the Georgia country's Hiwassee River) was placed between the layers of leather to protect the stump end of his amputated hand. It also gave Eli an added weapon.

With his gun hand on the ready, and somewhat shaky, Pete opened the front flap of the covered wagon. What he saw next caused his breakfast to come up. Eli had already cut the dog's throat from ear to ear. The slaver had rolled off the young girl while holding his throat, a futile attempt at stopping the blood flow. Hot, steaming blood was flying all over the back of the wagon. Eli cocked his head back and released an animalistic blood-curdling scream that chilled Pete to the bone.

When the chaos was over, Willow quickly entered the campsite to see to the wound on Joe's shoulder. As she was dressing the gunshot wound, she watched Eli's tender care of the young girl. Eli worked to care for this child with her mother's help once she was released from the chained group. Eli dressed her cuts while the child's mother treated her ripped vagina, then they got warm clothing for her. They impressed Willow.

The dead slavers had been moved out of the camp into the snow. They positioned the wagons as a windbreak making the camp cozier. As they consumed the cooked meat, each person's spirits started to lift. The slaves were glad to share their tragic stories.

The entire group had come from what they called "The Devil's Half Acre," which was Lumpkin's Slave Jail in Richmond, Virginia. They had departed as ten souls; two had died of disease, and another was killed while trying to escape. Robert Lumpkin, the jailer, had publicly whipped all but the children. They had all been half-starved.

Willow was surprised to learn that the raped young girl and her mother were slaves from the Berkeley Plantation on the James River, the birthplace of the president-elect William Henry Harrison. However, Willow was not surprised that the young girl claimed to be Harrison's daughter.

CHAPTER 16

The Poor House and Woodland Cemetery   August 1963   Ironton on the Ohio

My journey back from the night out at the tomb with the dead Indians was interesting, to put it mildly. While Grandma Wick sits here snoring and drawling in Shawnee spirit (and hopefully not burning this shotgun mansion down with her half-burning, kinnikinnick-filled pipe), I will try to catch you up on my journey back home.

Utilizing my sleep-deprived brain, I made a calculated, questionable, judgment call. I took a shortcut through Coal Grove near the Old Poor House (a place where my Grandma Lu always implied she would end up after my family bled her of every penny she had). She was our angel always going out on a limb by trying to help us.

I made another bold move and took another shortcut through the Woodland Cemetery rear gate, another place where Grandma Lu implied we were driving her to a quick nap with the worms. You should know by now that this detour through the haunted cemetery was a bold move for me. In fact, it was getting dark, and I am scared to death when I am near dead people that continue to walk this earth. I guarantee you that this was not my first rodeo in this cemetery.

My crew, the gang of dumb-asses, was warned in the past of the many ghosts that haunted this place. We always tried to convince ourselves that the stories were made up to scare us out of the cemetery. As for me, I had seen the ghost. I knew the stories were true. As if the haunting was not enough and the rules that did not allow kids on bikes at any time (nor kids without parents) to keep us out, the caretaker still had to chase me, Castle and Magoo out of this boneyard more times than I could count.

It was easy to get turned around in this place, but I had all the landmarks down to get through this boneyard in record time. The first landmark was a Masonic grave with the inscription "Whom Virtue Unites Death Cannot Separate" on the stone. The next marker was a mausoleum ornately decorated with an old photo of the Russian ballerina, Antoinette Peters. She was beautiful. A local legend has it that her ghost dances in this cemetery every night looking for her jewels. I know it's not a legend, I have seen her!

I made the right turn approaching the bridge over Ice Creek. In my brain, a voice was telling me to look over my shoulder. I couldn't help myself; I turned back for a look. I thought that my eyes and tired brain must be playing tricks on me. Standing about ten feet back, at the last grave, was my old Great-Grandma Wick with her arms outstretched.

Hitting the curb, I slammed the bike into the ground, shot over the handlebars, knocked the bark off my shin bones, and cracked my head into a small tree. My head was swimming with more visions. My only wish was that they would go away. Having been born under the veil (as told by the grandmas) made me somehow a soothsayer, a mystic like the shaman of the Shawnee. I always thought it was a crock of crap, but now I think I might have been wrong.

I knew this vision was a sign that she needed me at her house. She whispered in a musical Shawnee voice in my head as her image vanished then reappeared. I realized that I only knew a few words of the Shawnee language. Somehow, I understood all she had said to me, some of which came into my brain as a bloody picture that I wish I could forget. I kicked my bike into high gear and hauled ass. If you think I was scared shitless before, I can tell you that I was not any longer, because that load was in my pants.

The gatehouse caretaker was walking towards the massive iron gates, ready to lock down for the night. As I zoomed up behind him, he caught a glimpse of me on my wobbling bike. I was peddling all out to get through the gates before he could close them. The caretaker shut the first gate, then stepped into the second gate opening to block my exit. As I slowed to avoid a collision with him, he was able to grab the second gate. He had a look of real satisfaction on his face as the gates slammed together. He knew he had caught a big fish, not!

I made a quick cut and jumped over a hedgerow, sticking a four-point landing on the sidewalk leading to the pedestrian gate. I hit my funny bone on the gatepost numbing my left arm. As I hit the bricks on Lorain Street, I looked back to see the caretaker going ass over teakettle at the hedgerow. The look on his face was not nearly as satisfied. I rounded the corner at Fourth Street. On Lombard Elementary School's playground was the gang of dumb-asses: Magoo, Wiggy, Castle, and B. Ray all chanting, "Beaver! Beaver! Beaver!" So much for keeping secrets.

Arriving at Grandma Lu's screened back porch, I could see she was working to move the hanging medicine roots. She was shifting the snakeroot with the sassafras and ginseng root to allow even air flow. When dry she would make the medicines, first to take care of the family's needs, and then sell the remainder to the root shop on Center Street. I always looked carefully at what was hanging on that porch. Because, as my old pops said, "Look out for the scalps, shrunken heads, and nut sacks hanging on the old witch's back porch. Your scalp or nuts may be next!"

I told Grandma Lu of my night's adventure. She was astonished at my success. She had no faith that I would ever find the tomb. She wanted to know every detail: how I placed each item, the condition of the bones, and if I moved anything. *Oh, crap!* I didn't want to tell her I left the old rucksack. *What she didn't know couldn't hurt her, could it?* What I had in my pocket might cause her to shit a brick. For the first time, Grandma Lu looked at me with tears in her eyes and said, "Thanks." She doctored my wounds and sent me on my way to clean my shitty britches.

Grandma Wick was sleeping, so I returned to my house. The old man was on a boozed-up war path. He was drunk, as was the case most of the time during the summer. I was looking for a hole to hide in, praying he had forgotten about the blowout at the Wagoner's Bar. But he was still ticked at me about the incident.

As I was scrambling for a hideout, the old man blindsided me and knocked me off my feet right onto my shit-filled drawers. He was screaming that he was going to teach me how to keep my mouth shut, as if I couldn't keep a secret. My brain was spinning. All I could think of was that dripping beaver, and I started spilling my guts.

I told the full, vivid story of the beaver with that sweet, delicious oil mixture dripping off its golden pelt. I could see my daddy was visibly interested. Yet again, I should have kept my big mouth shut. I had given up the address in the details. The old man was going to take on this woman for the family's honor. He cut me some slack, looked at me and told me to clean my ass that I must have shit myself.

The next day I felt pretty darn good about myself, I had diverted a good ass kicking. *Maybe after my paper route, I will go and talk with Grandma Wick. Perhaps she could give me some understanding of what I had seen at the tomb and in the cemetery.*

I started my paper route. Things couldn't be going any better until I got to the house of the dripping beaver. I am not sure why, but I was shocked to see the old man's car there. I knew he was giving her an earful, upholding the Johnson family honor.

As the door opened, the old man stepped out onto her porch. I ducked behind a car across the street. I watched the woman come into view; the same robe was loose at the waist with oil and sweat projectiles shooting from the gap. The old man leaned in and put a lip lock on her that a crowbar couldn't break.

When the coast was clear, I ran like a wounded deer. *I don't think they saw me. I can't believe what just happened!* I realized the old man had filled up a lot more than her ear. At that point, I didn't know if I should laugh or cry. I just had a lot of pain for my poor momma. I guess what people had said about my daddy was true: he would screw a snake if someone would hold the head. Hell! That was the nicest thing they had said about him!

I began having nightmares that week. I just couldn't lose the visions I had at the Woodland Cemetery. My thoughts were that I was in some way the savior of the human race, especially when it involved roots. This entire mess was just not sitting well in my gut. It was too much for a pea-brain to digest. All the ghost stories flooded back to my mind after my ill-fated shortcut through that cemetery.

Thinking about what I saw that day, I tried to convince myself that the apparition I had seen was the Lady of Woodland ghost, not my great-grandmother. The lady was a ghost that stood watch at the entrance of the Woodland Cemetery. I always thought that tale was meant to keep punks like me out, now I had my doubts. Maybe, it was the object I had taken from Tecumseh's tomb talking to me. *Oh, heck! The curse is on!*

CHAPTER 17

The Great White Father's Inaugural   March 1841   Washington on the Potomac

Willow awoke in a comfortable bed refreshed for the first time since she parted from her home in South Point, Ohio. The beautiful farm was being used as an abolitionist safe-house for the movement of slaves. Located in the eastern mountains of Virginia, it now provided safe lodging for the weary travelers.

On their first journey as free people, the Lumpkin Jail slaves had a good night for the first time in their lives. Willow knew the pain in their hearts more than they could understand. With her burn-scarred face, damaged eye, and loss of her beloved family, she knew the horrors these people endured, as well as the pain of slavery.

Eli and Pete had taken care of the dead Lumpkin Jail slavers. They severed the heads, arms, and legs, and gutted the bodies, scattering the parts to the four winds for the wolves to feast on as no man should remember these devils. Joe's shoulder wound would prevent him from going with them to the inauguration. He was disappointed but would serve as a valuable resource by helping the farm family aid the freed people.

The weather warmed for the trip twenty-three miles north of Martin's farm to the ferry dock on the Chesapeake & Ohio Canal. The canal flatboat was loaded with people trying to arrive in Washington before the inauguration on March 4, 1841. All of the travelers on board, except Willow's group, carried some type of banner for the old hero of Tippecanoe supporting his rise to the seat of the Great White Father.

Willow wished she could show them the real vision of the massacre of the Shawnee people and her family on the Tippecanoe. The image of that sacred river running red with their life blood was etched forever in her mind. Willow's group was fortunate to get passage on this boat, mayhap their appearance caused some to step aside. The passengers looked at Willow with her burn-scarred face and dead eye as though she was a demon. As if Willow's appearance wasn't enough to satisfy their morbid curiosities, they turned and gawked at Eli, who looked like an Indian mule skinner with one hand missing.

Eli looked them in the eye and snarled, sounding like his dog Copper. He was wearing a buckskin coat and britches, and had a cluster of eagle feathers dangling from his buckskin hat. He also had his instruments of death (a tomahawk and a blood-stained knife) sheathed to his side. Needless to say, people gave him a lot of space when they saw him. His appearance may have caused some of the men to piss their trousers.

The group had a run of trouble halfway down the river. The boat they were in collided with an iced-over rock and took on water. This caused them to transfer to another canal boat. The remainder of the journey went well.

Willow's group arrived at the falls of the Potomac after dark on the second day where they were met by a Masonic Brother. He had anticipated their arrival earlier, but their safety was his reward. They traveled by coach from the falls to Georgetown where Masonic Brothers greeted them at the warm safe-house. This beautiful place was within a comfortable walk to the White House where all the inaugural activities would take place.

Willow awoke on the first day of March, three days before the inauguration. She occupied her time by catching up on the backlog of newspapers brought to the safe-house. Willow learned of the old general's retreat to the family's Berkeley Plantation on the James River in Virginia. She read about the flood of cabinet post selections and other significant positions given to Whig Party members.

Old Tippecanoe had made the rounds from Frederick, Maryland where he boarded a train that carried him and his entourage to Baltimore. There were great celebrations at each stop along the way. The train traveled on to

Washington. At each whistle stop, he received a hero's welcome and was given gifts of exquisite coaches, clothing, and furs.

Some news articles referenced bad omens such as the late season snowfall that signaled his arrival in Baltimore. And the fall of the Senate Chamber scroll bearing the motto "E Pluribus Unum." Also, upon Harrison's arrival in Washington, the rope bearing the flags of the states that had given a majority vote for his election as president that spanned Pennsylvania Avenue, had broken. All of these facts reported by opposition newspapers were noted by Willow.

Willow realized that this was not nearly as prophetic an omen as the one she had seen in the morning sky. While enjoying the early morning light in the sky over Washington, she saw the distinct tail of the Panther in the Sky; the sign of which the great leader Tecumseh was born and named. This tail appeared to point straight to the location of the White House.

Willow was now sure of the reason for the selling of the Berkeley Plantation slaves. After the vicious attacks on Vice President Johnson's character, the Whig Party was forced to bury Harrison's misadventures with the family slaves. The thought of the raped, young girl possibly being his daughter left a sick feeling in her gut.

Harrison's greed was most likely the secondary reason for paying off his campaign debt. Lumpkin's Jail served his and the Whig Party's need for a secret dumping ground for the human flesh. Harrison's hands were more than blood-stained.

The second day of March arrived with news that the old general had returned to the nation's Capital from his seclusion at the Berkeley Plantation. With him was his white daughter, Anna Taylor. His daughter-in-law, Jane Findlay Harrison, would serve as White House hostess as Harrison's wife was ill and staying at North Bend in Ohio.

On this morning, Willow had taken a long walk. She wished to be alone to clear her mind. She was surprised when she realized she was on Pennsylvania Avenue. Willow looked up to see a commotion just ahead and was shocked to see the president-elect, William Henry Harrison, walking in her direction.

Harrison was walking with a slight limp, a cane in his left hand. He was using his right hand to shake hands and was bowing to the women. A military escort of three followed about ten feet behind him. Pennsylvania Avenue was abuzz with supporters swirling around this evil man. In the newspaper articles, the Democrats had warned of the multitude of Whig pocket pickers who made the early morning walks with Harrison and robbed everyone in sight. They were busy on this day.

Willow had a moment of panic, then thought that she was not the one who needed to panic. She would not bolt and run like a deer in the sights of a hunter. Willow would never back down from this dog again. She decided to walk directly towards him, look the devil in the evil eye and pray that he would not rob her soul.

Willow walked with her head held high. The old general was busy greeting his multitude of hurrahing supporters. As he passed her, he extended his right hand without looking. When she did not accept his greeting, he looked up. The look on his face was as if he had seen a ghost. He had recognized her. Willow continued walking, she looked back only after she passed the soldiers.

Harrison had turned looking at her with his mouth gaped open, clearly wanting to say something, but the words would not come out. This from a man, no a windbag, who was never short of words. He was now animatedly talking to the confused soldiers while pointing in Willow's direction. As she crossed the street, with the wind at her back, she was quickly lost in the gathering of the crowd. She hit a side street and vanished. Like a ghost, she was gone.

Willow arrived at the safe-house winded yet excited from looking into the eyes of the devil himself. Eli could see and feel her joyous excitement. He wanted to hear all the details with one thought in mind: *Could I get that close to kill Harrison with one blow of my tomahawk and send his brains flying into the crowd of his adoring fans?* Willow was praying she could persuade Eli to change his mind from killing this man by letting the letters she brought help bring Harrison down.

Willow had a surprise for Eli, which might soften his heart and change his mind from his murderous design. She held his hand in her two strong hands, looked him in the eyes, and told him she would need him now more than ever because the Great Good Spirit has again blessed them with child. With him dead or in jail she could not survive. Life would be meaningless without him.

Willow, now forty-two summers old, knew this was most likely their last chance to have a family to carry on their bloodline. A family to live to tell the true stories of their Shawnee and Cherokee people. Eli's great joy from this news dampened the burning desire he had to gain revenge. Willow felt this burden lift from her soul.

Inaugural Day dawned cold and damp with a brisk northeast wind. More than a dozen bands played, military units marched, and students from the Jesuit College at Georgetown paraded past the old general. The old Tippecanoe units riding on horse-drawn floats waved at the early morning crowds.

Harrison rode on his favorite horse, Whitey. Trying to show off his vigor, he did not wear an overcoat, gloves, or hat. He was bowing and waving at the crowd, which included Willow and her entourage. Eli was rubbing the handle of his tomahawk while visualizing it cracking old Tippecanoe's skull into two parts with the brains splashing all over Whitey.

Vice President Tyler was sworn into office just before noon on the fourth day of March while Harrison watched. Tyler gave a brief speech. Harrison then exited the Senate Chamber with a slight bow towards the gathering of dignitaries. Harrison stood on the outdoor platform assessing the crowd. There were more than fifty thousand shivering Americans wanting to see and hear this great man who had attained his power from the weak. He wanted to show them his power, vim, and vigor by not wearing a hat, gloves or overcoat.

Harrison thought this would be an inaugural speech to remember for ages to come, a chance of a lifetime for these miserable wretches. In the shivering multitude was a motley group of Indians praying for help from the wave of forced removals from their homelands. There was also a number of southern states represented with people wanting the right to control their slave ownership or to secede from this union of states. With this president, they thought there was a good chance they could accomplish all their goals.

Willow and her group were little different. They wished to hear good news for the beleaguered Indian tribes and a great desire to see someone step up with a conscious mind to abolish slavery. They only needed to continue to listen, in the cold, to this windbag's two hour and forty-five-minute diatribe to get their answers.

Harrison's inaugural address rambled on. The newspapers reported before the speech that Daniel Webster had attempted to change much of this diatribe windbag's criticisms of beliefs. The beliefs in how the government formed this great nation and the undertones of the Masonic hand in all aspects of the founders. However, he failed. Harrison was losing the crowd. A vast majority of those gathered began to gossip about the rumored appointments. There were also stories of Henry Clay calling for an extra session of Congress to establish a new United States Bank. The country was broke after years of depression.

Harrison regained the crowd's attention with a subject that he held strong convictions for, "Congress had no right to abolish slavery in the District of Columbia." He reiterated, "...without the consent of the people therein. Our citizens must be content with the exercise of powers with which the Constitution clothes them. The attempt of those of one state to control the domestic institutions of another can only result in feelings of distrust and jealousy, the certain harbingers of disunions, violence and civil war..."

There it was. The slave state crowd let out a cheer of approval for almost two minutes. Willow and her group of confirmed abolitionists looked at each other with a level of understanding that not many in the multitude had. They had access to Harrison's letters that entailed the evil plans formed years earlier by Harrison, Jackson, and Jefferson.

There were many tribal representatives from across the nation in attendance. Like Willow and the group that she had traveled with to this event, they wanted the address to relate to their concerns. Concerns for the thousands of native people being removed from their land. Their lives and land being stolen.

Harrison finally stopped speaking, cleared his throat and went on to the subject of the Indians. "In our intercourse with our Aboriginal neighbors, the same liberality and justice, which marked the course prescribed to me by two of my illustrious predecessors when acting under their direction in the discharge of the duties of superintendent and commissioner, shall be strictly observed. I can conceive of no more sublime spectacle, none more likely to propitiate an impartial and common Creator, than a rigid adherence to the principles of justice on the part of a powerful nation in its transactions with a weaker and uncivilized people whom circumstances have placed at its disposal..."

Willow was slack-jawed. She could see the blood boiling in Eli's veins when she looked at him. She took his hand just as he was reaching for his tomahawk. Eli's English was as good as Willow's. They knew the meaning of this windbag's evil message to the Indian people.

Willow's thoughts and beliefs were that there would be no change in the treatment of the native population. She felt Harrison would continue to kill and steal the lands, customs, and religion of these honest people as prescribed by Presidents Jackson and Jefferson. President Jackson had once said that the only good Indian was a dead Indian.

President Jefferson guided Harrison's hand when Harrison was Territorial Governor. He made Harrison a success by enslaving or massacring the Indian population of the Northwest Territories. The Indians who lived there have been civilized for more than fifteen thousand years. Willow knew it would take all her effort to stop Eli from murdering this man and spreading his guts to the four winds. But in her heart, she was not sure she wanted to stop him.

Chief Justice Roger B. Taney administered the presidential oath of office to Harrison. Harrison then saluted the crowd with his fare thee well. His Negro slave arrived to assist him with his hat and cloak. The military boomed a final salute as their new leader departed for the White House. Willow was shocked to see old George on the platform assisting Harrison with his coat. She now knew that Harrison intended to show his disregard for the anti-slavery contingent in the crowd by this display of arrogance.

Willow and her group returned to the safe-house in Georgetown. Their discussion was heated concerning the way to take care of Harrison. Would the letters do enough damage or was Eli's plan the way to go? At the White House on Pennsylvania Avenue, the new president was laying down for a short nap as his slave rubbed his head and temples with alcohol. The lower floor of the White House mansion was full of well-wishers and office seekers waiting for the inaugural ball to begin. All was good in the old general's life, or so he thought.

CHAPTER 18
Greasing the Wheels of the Presidential Coach to Hell
April 1841 Washington on the Potomac

The White House was a beehive of activity for two weeks after the inaugural ceremony. The spoils system was overpowering and consuming much of Harrison's time. Partisan appointees from previous presidential administrations were reviewed to protect public funds. A few years before, a Jackson appointee had stolen a cool million dollars. Harrison did not want the embarrassment from a repeat of this type of public greed.

Two incidents consumed a great deal of Harrison's time: A war of letters with Henry Clay of Kentucky concerning a special session of Congress, and that of the American vessel, the Caroline. The latter of which had a good outcome by avoiding war with England. This resolution was gratifying for Harrison's first two weeks in office. He hoped his visits to every department would be as successful.

Harrison met with the delegations of Indian tribes on the White House lawn. Discussions centered around their removal from their native lands. All they received from Harrison were more lies. The same type they had gotten for the last two hundred years.

Willow and Eli followed Harrison as he did his early morning marketing with White House hostess Jane Findlay at his side. Mrs. Harrison was continuing to recover in Ohio. They slowly walked down Pennsylvania Avenue with only two federal soldiers in tow, ten feet behind with their guns at rest. Eli thought about how easy it would be to let out a blood-curdling scream, run to Harrison's side, and split his skull open before the soldiers could get off a shot. In Eli's head, Willow's voice was telling him not to risk their lives and the lives of their children for the joy of killing this dog.

Willow and Eli had Harrison's routine down better than his White House staff. The only exception was old George, who was always at the president's side. On Sunday, you could always find old Tippecanoe in pew number forty-five at St. John's Episcopal Church located at 16th and H Streets. Old George, his Negro slave, was standing outside with Harrison's overcoat, hat and cane in hand like a faithful dog patiently awaiting its master's return.

Pete and Ike had made some important Masonic contacts in Georgetown, who could use the letters Willow brought to help bring this president down. On the morning of March 27, 1841, Willow, Pete, and Ike had finally convinced Eli that killing Harrison was the wrong path to take. Stripping him of his power would be more punishment than the old general could stand. He would then most likely commit suicide, which would solve all of their concerns.

Pete and Ike had taken ill with a spring flu on this rainy morning. Willow had old Uncle Yellow Robe's medicine bag and mixed an ancient remedy for the group. It would take effect in about two days, along with good bed rest. She also went to the market to try and find the spring greens and herbs to make a Shawnee spring elixir that would clean out the lower bowels. Tall Walker Woman always said, "Keep the bottom open, and the top will take care of itself."

Willow made the short walk to the market using an umbrella for protection from the cold March rain. This was the first time she had used an umbrella and was fascinated with the utility of this white man's invention. She thought of the greater good that might have been if the white man would have integrated with the Indian people in harmony. They could have learned to live together: sharing their land, ideas, medicines, and cultures.

Willow arrived at the market to find it nearly empty due to the cold rain, which kept people home. She took the large medicine bag with her, as it had plenty of space for the herbs and greens she would carry back with her. Willow drifted through the market, not only finding the herbs and spring greens required for the Shawnee spring elixir but some of the rare medicine herbs needed for her remedies as well. She was surprised because she started having trouble finding some of them in the Ohio woodlands.

Willow was bent over a large basket of ginseng root when she heard a familiar voice from her past. "Ciicothe," he said in a soft-spoken voice. It was her good friend old George. They embraced like long lost family members that had not seen each other for years and were finally reunited. Willow and George were in a trance of conversation concerning her escape from North Bend and the years as a free person, oblivious to the activity and danger around them.

Old George was pushed to the ground as Willow was grabbed by each arm from behind. She dropped her old medicine bag as she struggled in a useless effort to break the soldier's grip. President Harrison walked towards them when the area was clear. Willow was making an attempt to calm down. Harrison was carrying a handkerchief, wiping at the snot running from his raw nose. Willow could see he was sick from the grippe that was running its course in the Washington D.C. area.

Harrison leaned into Willow's face, she could smell death on his breath. In an angry voice, he said, "I want my papers returned, or someone will die." Willow was forcibly hauled out of the market and jerked violently towards the jail. She could resist and maybe break free, but all she could think of was the safety of her unborn child. Willow was angry at her mistake. She knew Harrison would not be far from old George, his prized slave. She now worried that this blunder could cost them the overall mission or mayhap her life.

Harrison walked angrily through the rain ignoring the umbrella that old George was trying to hold over his head that would have given him some protection from the cold March weather. Old George limped in an effort to stay in stride with Harrison. The president walked with a mission in mind to offer a diplomatic post to his friend Colonel John Tayloe, Master of the Octagon House on Lafayette Square. Harrison's thoughts were of Ciicothe, getting his letters returned, and his reputation protected.

That evening Harrison dined with Colonel Tayloe, Morton Bradley (a guest of the colonel's from Illinois) and other office seekers. Before he could complete the meal, he was forced to retire to his bed in the White House and a physician was summoned. Due to the age of the president, bleeding was not employed. Instead, he was liberally cupped. Nothing they tried helped. His fever continued to increase with acute symptoms of pneumonia and intestinal inflammation. The physician diagnosed Harrison's condition as bilious pleurisy.

Eli's rage could not be contained when he learned of Willow's capture and her subsequent incarceration in the capital jail. When she failed to return, Pete went to the market looking for her. The manager who witnessed the incident with the president's troops told Pete what had happened. Eli did not sleep that night. It was Sunday, March 28, and he knew he could find Harrison in pew number forty-five in St. John's Episcopal Church. Someone was going to die.

Eli arrived at 16th and H Streets as the last of the communicants entered the church. People who passed by the one-handed, war-painted Indian with a blood-caked tomahawk in his hand quickly crossed to the opposite side of the street. Eli saw two soldiers standing near the door acting as if nothing was bothering them. They tried to ignore his approach, but Eli raised his face to the heavens and let out a scream from hell that caused one of the soldiers to piss his britches.

One soldier tried to level his gun, but before he could, Eli's tomahawk cracked his skull like a ripe melon. The soldier with the piss-stained britches attempted to hit Eli with the butt of his gun without success; he was knocked out with one blow. Eli kicked open the massive oaken doors of the church, the noise woke the congregation. Eli's eyes looked at the unoccupied pew number forty-five. He let out another blood-curdling scream, which caused a panic of the people in the church to seek cover in any direction available.

Eli stepped back into the daylight thinking only of his destination, the White House. He didn't see the piss-stained soldier who had recovered from the strike of the tomahawk. The soldier drew his weapon, fired at close range, and hit Eli in the head. Eli went down like a sack of potatoes. The light in his eyes slowly faded. Eli heard the hunting drums of his Cherokee people in the beautiful Appalachian Mountains, a happier time. That delirium faded into blackness.

Willow suffered seven days of hell in the capital jail. She had little food or water, and the sanitary conditions were deplorable. The treatment of the horses in the attached barns was much better than what Willow had received. She had an overflowing slop bucket that did not get emptied for several days; her clothing was soiled and torn. She was spotting blood; she thought she was going to miscarry her baby.

Willow's misery was compounded by the story circulating through the jail of a crazy Indian going nuts on the steps at St. John's Episcopal Church. A one-handed, wild Indian had murdered seven people before being killed by a brave soldier. Lucky for the Washington population that the soldier was there awaiting the president's arrival, who, fortunately, was a no-show for this Sunday service.

Willow knew from the description of the crazy Indian that it could be none other than her beloved Eli. He had gone nuts when he heard about Willow's capture. She also knew his target was the president. Her heart hurt with the thought of her love, Eli, dead.

The guards' arrival broke her morbid chain of thought. They surprised her with clean clothes and fresh water. They also allowed her to clean herself in advance of a forthcoming mystery visitor. She was more surprised at the visitor's identity than she was with the guards' arrival. The visitor was Jane Findlay Harrison.

The arrival of Jane Findlay Harrison (the widow of William Jr. and presiding White House hostess) at this filthy jail was a shock. Jane Findlay described the president's dire medical condition. She described his adamant request to bring Willow to his bedside.

Willow arrived at the White House rear entrance, which is used exclusively for servants. Her old friend George welcomed her with a hug. He was sorry for her grief, which he felt like he had caused at the market. She could see he had been crying for his ill master, but her heart felt no sorrow for the evil man Harrison.

There was food on the large kitchen table that they had prepared for her. Water was boiling on the cooktop of an enormous stove. Willow's old medicine bag (given to her so many years ago by Uncle Yellow Robe) was placed on a small, side table. She now knew what they wanted of her. They expected her to save the life of this dog.

Willow had been allowed to eat, and then quickly taken to the bedroom of the president. She was introduced to Doctor Worthington, who stared at her burn-scarred face as if she was the most grotesque thing he had ever seen. Harrison's minister completed reading the 103rd Psalm, *"Bless the Lord, all his works, in all the places of God's dominion, Bless the Lord, O my Soul."* Once he finished, Harrison asked everyone to leave the room except Willow.

In a weak voice, Harrison asked Willow to step closer to his bed. She did so and could smell death on this man. She could see the effects of disease and a weak poison slowly killing this evil man. Harrison pled, "Ah, Ciicothe, I am ill, very ill, much more so than the doctors think I am. I need you to make the remedy that saved John Scot's life so many years ago on the Miami at North Bend." Willow did not have to put much thought into this request; she departed the room on a mission.

Back in the kitchen, with a doctor looking over her shoulder, Willow started brewing a remedy. The potion was not to save this dog but to add some grease to the wheels on his journey to hell. Harrison would get his payday for Eli's death. As she concocted the brew, she couldn't help but laugh to herself. The importance of his worthless papers in her care did not cross Harrison's lips.

Willow made the brew with such particular care that the hapless doctor had not a clue as to what it would do. Willow reflected on the prophecies from Tecumseh's spirit concerning the dog Mad Anthony Wayne, and the braves who carried death to that evil man. She knew that Harrison's death may be her reward.

Against Doctor Worthington's better judgment, the poisoned tea brew was taken to Harrison's room. He had Willow drink a large dose first. She coughed, all the while smiling. Seeing that she survived, he was satisfied. Harrison consumed it greedily, stating he felt better almost instantly with a weak smile on his distorted face. Willow knew this death was not as dramatic as a tomahawk to the skull, but this would be more painful.

Willow was surprised to be allowed to depart. Doctor Worthington told her that he did not trust her witch doctor remedies, but they had to respect the president's wishes. What the good doctor failed to say, was that he and the other four physicians attending the president had no clue how to save this old man; they didn't care if she put him out of his misery. It would give them a scapegoat, someone to blame.

Willow had a tearful goodbye with old George. She told him that a home in South Point, Ohio awaited him and his family if he ever got his freedom and that her door would always be open to them. Willow made her exit with only seconds to spare before projectile vomiting her guts out. She made the short run to the safe-house, vomiting every few steps.

Willow was shocked and elated to find Pete and Ike trying to save Eli's life. He was in a coma with a crack in his skull from the iron shot that could not penetrate his hard head. Her priority was to make an antidote for the small amount of poison in her system. She did not have her old medicine bag so she would have to make do with what she had gotten from the market.

Pete and Ike told Willow about how they found Eli laying in the street in such horrible condition. He had appeared dead. However, as they lifted his head, he groaned. In the panic and confusion at the church, they carried him to this place where their attempt to nurse him back to health seemed destined to fail.

Willow was sick. She continued to dry retch from the poison she had ingested. She ignored her condition, although she worried for her unborn child. Willow was going to give all her effort to saving Eli. She could feel that he had a strong spirit to live.

At six o'clock on Saturday, April 3, Doctor Worthington was in the White House. He and the four attending physicians agreed that the president was beyond recovery. Harrison had degraded into a stupor of delirium. His once sharp mind wandered in unclear thought, there was froth gurgling from his mouth, and a foul odor coming from his body. Death came on Sunday, the fourth of April at twelve-thirty.

Doctor Worthington heard the president's last words, "Sir, I wish you to understand the true principles of the government. I wish them carried out. I ask for nothing more." The doctor thought this odd; mayhap a prayer for his soul might have been more appropriate, mayhap this was more delirium.

The official death report read: Topical depletion, blistering and appropriate internal remedies, subdued in a great measure, the disease of the lungs and liver, but the stomach and intestines did not regain a healthy condition. A portion of the report that would never be revealed contained a suggestion that poison was taken voluntarily, provided by an Indian Shaman confidant of unknown origin. This part of the report the good doctor would keep secret, close to the vest in an effort to cover his own ass.

CHAPTER 19

Two Funerals September 1963 Ironton on the Ohio

Ah, September was here, and everyone longed for that autumn cool down and the kickoff of Ironton Fighting Tiger football. But that was not happening, the summer heat was hanging around. Magoo, Castle and I had taken a dip in our favorite, big, swanky swimming hole, Ice Creek. This creek was one you had to be very careful of and always stay upstream of the cement plant and the other nasty industries that dumped filthy wastewater into it. If you took a dip in the wrong place, you risked losing all your hair, skin, and God only knew what else.

"Hey Magoo, did I tell you the story of my Indian uncle, Chief Bowels?" I didn't wait for his answer, I was going to tell this story even if he knew it by heart. Uncle Bowels lived on a reservation in Oklahoma where he owned some valuable land that the white man wanted. They sent a government agent known by the tribesmen as the silver-tongued devil.

Chief Bowels' English was poor. When they started negotiations, he had trouble understanding. But at the end of each meeting, he always said emphatically, "Bowels no move!" After a week of these meetings, the agent got sick. The tribe thought Bowels was also ill. The tribal doctor went to Bowels' teepee. The chief (thinking that this was the agent's replacement) continued to exclaim, "Bowels no move!" The doctor thought Bowels was constipated and started treating him with a strong laxative.

For the next week Bowels continued to state that he would not move and the doctor continued to give Bowels more of the laxative. The tribe could hear strange noises coming from Bowels' wigwam, "Oh, oh, oh, ugh, ugh," with sounds of massive farting. The doctor came the next day, Chief Bowels came out looking pale. Defeated, Chief Bowels looked at the doctor (who he thought was the land agent) exclaiming "Bowels got to move, wigwam full of shit!"

As we headed home, our gang of dumb-asses could chalk up another wasted day. I felt awful for telling that sad joke and wished I could somehow take it back when my brother Bubby came running towards us. He looked very agitated and was crying like a baby. He broke my heart that day with the bad news he delivered, news I had expected for several weeks.

My Grandma Wick had died. I had a series of bad dreams that had haunted my nights for two weeks prior to her passing. These dreams had foretold of her death. She had been ill most of the summer and had gotten a severe nose bleed earlier in the week that could not be controlled by their old Indian methods.

As was my grandmas' routine, they tried to treat at home with their old Indian remedies. Going to a hospital or doctor was out of the question. That was considered a luxury. They had no extra money for that frivolous crap, "Get another root!" was the Indian battle cry. I was told that due to her advanced age she died of natural causes. *How the heck is not having health care a natural cause?*

Now, being the selfish dog that I am, I only thought of not getting to hear the remainder of the story about my Grandma Ciicothe Reed's life. At least I knew that she had accomplished her mission in Washington D.C. by killing that dog Harrison. But possibly never knowing the details of their return adventure to Ohio was bugging the crap out of me.

Grandma Wick was only a few weeks from her ninety-second birthday. Born in 1872 she had seen a lot of living. Her father James Tecumseh Reed served with the Ohio 33rd Infantry during the Civil War. Her son Art served in World War I and her grandson Bubby served in both World War II and the Korean War.

My grandma saw the world change from horse and buggy to automobiles, man taking to the air like birds (in airplanes then jets), the Great

Depression, and so much more than I will ever know. What a fascinating life she must have had! I regretted not talking more with Grandma Wick concerning her life. As it is with most young people, I was self-centered. I only thought about my own pleasures.

My family had assembled at Grandma Lu's house on the evening of the funeral home visit and memorial service. Grandma Lu and my mom had made extra food as if we were celebrating some big event, but I was way too sad to eat. My brother Bubby had vomited three times and was shaking like a dog shitting razor blades. He was very nervous about going to the funeral home.

I could smell the smoky remnants of the kinnikinnick tobacco that Grandma Wick had been burning in her old, stone, Indian pipe when I last sat in the living room listening to her tell the incredible story of Willow Ciicothe Reed. I had my eyes closed and could see her sitting in her old chair with blood covering the walls; I was starting to freak myself out! I was snapped back to reality by Grandma Lu's gentle touch on the back of my head as she whispered, "Things will work out."

Wilber arrived in his old, black, custom Super 8 Packard with its massive bird hood ornament guiding that huge hood. Web (as we called him) was a longtime family friend who was always ready to help. Web relieved a lot of the tension in the house with his jolly attitude.

My old man was not going to attend Grandma Wick's funeral because, as he said, "They would have crazy Indian witch doctors blowing smoke or other weird shit," so he stayed home with my seven brothers and sisters who were all too young to go to the memorial service. He was probably getting drunk on Miller, waiting for our return home with some ass-kicking in mind for all of us.

I jumped into the middle of the old Packard's back seat with my younger brother Mike and my sister Beverly. Riding shotgun was Bubby on my right and our sister Sharon on my left. Oh yes! You can fit five kids in the back seat of a Packard, and most likely have some extra space for some farm animals in that big car! My beloved Mom and Grandma Lu sat in the front seat with Web as he drove. He dropped the Packard into gear, the car lurched forward, and we were on our way. *Phillips Funeral Home, here we come!*

When we arrived, I could see the reason why they called this place a home. It was nothing but a large fancy house used for dead people. I had never seen a dead person, except on one rare hang out with Bubby and his main, run-around gal Jennie. We walked the Ohio riverbank looking for some trouble to get into. We had stolen a whole, raw chicken and was going to have a mud-roasted yard bird picnic.

We came upon a bum washed up on the shore of the Ohio riverbank, and we thought he was dead. Bubby got a long stick and started poking the body. There was no reaction from the bum. Bubby and Jennie got close and leaned in to get a better look. I was too afraid to go any closer than five feet.

Suddenly, the old hobo raised up, farted, and let out a heart-stopping scream; a wine bottle fell to the ground. Jennie dropped the chicken, and we ran like the wind until we got to the Center Street flood wall exit. We did not look back until we made the turn. The bum had gotten up, with the raw chicken in his hand. He was looking at it as if it was a gift from God. That wino ate well that night!

We entered the funeral home, and I moved as slow as a crippled turtle towards the coffin. I was afraid, praying for my Grandmother Wick's soul. I also prayed that she would not sit up in that coffin and grab me, causing me to soil myself. I was not sure if my legs would hold up; my knees were knocking like a baseball card in a bicycle wheel's spokes.

Both my Mom and Grandma Lu had tears flowing. Now, I will tell you my Mom cried at the drop of a hat. But this may have only been the second time I ever saw a tear in my Grandma Lu's eyes. She was one tough woman. She was raised hard through two World Wars and the Great Depression, which also took my grandfather's life on the N & W Railroad tracks. His death forced my grandma to raise her three children alone. With Indian toughness, she could put a hairy eyeball on you that could turn you to stone and make a dumb-ass like me think twice about getting into trouble.

The funeral service was now over. Bubby had a puke attack during the eulogy, having to run outside. I am not sure where he found anything in his guts to hurl, but he did. He unloaded it on the front porch of this beautiful house. Just a guess, but this would most likely be Bubby's first and last funeral until the undertaker is preparing him for his own funeral.

We returned to Grandma Lu's house in Web's Packard. Everyone was sitting in the living room, having a pleasant conversation and reminiscing sentimentally about our Grandma Wick's life when a car horn started to continuously honk at the front of the house. We looked out the windows and were shocked to see the old man in his 1956 Chevy Sedan loaded to the headliner with the rest of the Johnson tribe.

To no surprise, the old man was drunk. He got out of the car holding Carl Paul by the straps of his bib overalls. (Carl Paul was the baby of the family and not yet two years old.) The baby was dangling off the ground like a twenty-pound bag of spuds. Mom ran out the door. As she approached the car, dad tossed little Carl Paul into the air. Luckily, she caught him in mid-flight like a football. They got in each other's faces and began arguing.

The old man raised his hand to hit Mom. I ran for the back door and grabbed the wood hatchet with intentions of killing him. This was not a good day for me to see the old man put a beat-down on my Mom. *I will split his skull, and we will be attending funeral number two.*

As I rounded the corner of the house, someone had extended their arm and clotheslined my dumb ass, and the hatchet went flying to the ground. While lying flat on my back, I thought the old man was about to end my life with one swift kick to the throat. I looked up, only to see my Grandma Lu picking up her old hatchet. She had that look in her eye. The same look I had seen a few months before when she intended to kill me with that same hatchet. She turned hell-bent for the front yard.

After pulling myself together, (I felt like I was a skinny running back who had just taken a beat-down from a two hundred fifty-pound linebacker) I staggered into the front yard. Grandma Lu was standing with the hatchet in her hand and there was no blood dripping off of it. *The old man is safe for now.*

Dad was pulling away after unloading the rest of my brothers and sisters. He was headed for a night of drunken bliss. Maybe he would be gone all night, allowing our family to grieve in peace. The old man will never know how close we came to having a second funeral that day.

Our family bunked down in Grandma Lu's small shotgun house that night. The next morning she was up early making an oven full of cathead biscuits. On the cooktop were two large iron skillets boiling brown sausage gravy. I had gotten up early to help, but Bubby had beat me out of the fart sack. He was already stirring the gravy. We finished eating, and I helped with cleanup.

Grandma Lu sensed my sadness. After breakfast, she apologized for the block she had put on me. She asked if I wanted to hear the rest of the story about Grandma Reed's life. "Yes," I replied. I thought the story had gone to the grave with my Grandma Wick.

Looking me in the eye, Grandma Lu said, "Don't worry, I know the story by heart." Even better, she was with her Grandma Reed when she died at Willow's Woods. Eli's clear stone that I had pilfered and removed from the tomb started to pulse in my pocket. A lightning bolt of pain ricocheted through my head. *I dare not share this information with my Grandma Lu, or my ass will be grass, and she will be the lawn mower!*

CHAPTER 20

The Journey Home   May 1841   South Point and North Bend on the Ohio

Daniel Webster had dispatched his son Fletcher to notify Vice President Tyler (who was presently in Williamsburg, Virginia) of President Harrison's untimely death. Word of the president's death had spread quickly. Few people knew of his extended illness; many in the population were shocked by the news. Washington was in deep mourning; banners of black replaced the inaugural badges on Pennsylvania Avenue. All private homes had black crape hanging on the door knockers or over the transoms.

The Washington and other newspapers carried editorials of woe and despair for the president. Many citizens of Washington remembered seeing the president (a robust, older man) walking to the market on Pennsylvania Avenue only two weeks before his death. Some people recalled the bad omens upon his February arrival. Now the rumor of an assassination by poison was running amongst the citizens of the capital city like a wildfire through a hayfield.

Willow was at the Georgetown safe-house giving all of her effort to saving Eli's life. She would not join in mourning for the president. Willow was sad for Harrison's family but had only one concern: that someone may have partially poisoned Harrison before she gave him his final boost into hell. Now she would not be able to take full credit for the revenge killing of this evil man.

Pete and Ike knew nothing of the poisoning, nor of Willow's exploits to get free from the capital jail. The thoughts of revenge they had towards this man became mute, and their Masonic belief in God now guided their judgment. Harrison's eternal fate and final judgment were now in the hands of the Great Architect of the Universe.

The president's body was laid to rest in the east room of the White House. All areas of this magnificent structure were shrouded in black. Harrison lay in a glass-lid coffin covered with velvet. The president looked peaceful, flowers filled the room. Inside the east room, the rector of St. John's Episcopal Church read selections from the Bible. He reminisced of Harrison's church-going ways and love of reading the Bible.

On Wednesday, April 7, volunteer marine and artilleryman companies assembled on Pennsylvania Avenue; cannons were fired. Harrison's favorite horse, old Whitey (saddled and riderless), was last in the procession. Thousands waited to pay their respects at the Capitol where the president's body would stay before its long journey west to North Bend on the Ohio.

Pete and Ike were needed to assist loading Eli into the covered wagon. His physical recovery was complete, but his mental status was unchanged. He could not speak, nor could he recognize people. Willow would take him home to Ohio while continuing to pray for his recuperation. Willow's near poisoning from her own brew was easing in her gut and the retching had slowed. She could now hold down some nourishment.

The bad weather had let up, which made traveling on the Cumberland Pike possible. Joe, with the support of the abolitionists, had departed with the freed Lumpkin's Jail slaves for Ohio earlier in the month. After hearing about the death of Harrison, he knew it was important to change locations. Willow and her group were in need of some good luck while traveling to make their rendezvous with the Ben Franklin steamboat in Brownsville on the Monongahela.

They arrived in Brownsville on Saturday, April 17, with one day to spare before the departure of the Ben Franklin. As they approached the loading dock, Willow's group could sense something was different. The crowd was numbered in the thousands. Ike went to see what was going on. When he returned, he told them that the flatboat was reserved for President Harrison's body and the funeral party. The crowd had assembled to see him off, which added more insult to injury from this evil man, even in his death.

Horse-drawn coaches began to arrive. They carried Harrison's body, the family, and the rest of the funeral party. The crowd wore black armbands and was hushed for respect as the funeral coach that carried the body of the president had arrived. Sitting next to the driver on Harrison's coach was his old, Negro slave George. The coffin was transferred to the deck of the boat. As the Harrison family and the funeral party boarded, Jane Findlay saw Willow and looked her directly in the eye. With great agitation, she tried to point Willow out to a soldier. Willow vanished into the crowd.

Willow and her group boarded the next flatboat. Departing Brownsville on the next steamboat, the American, they were only a few miles behind the Ben Franklin. At each port along the Ohio River, mourners remained lined on the riverbanks and docks as they passed. The spring flow of this beautiful river was carrying them home at a record pace.

On the evening of Tuesday, April 20, 1841, Willow arrived at the David's ferry dock at South Point, Ohio. She could no longer hide the fact that she was pregnant. Hiram was excited to see them. He was overjoyed by Willow's condition. Willow was grateful to God that the poison she ingested did not kill her unborn baby.

Hiram had always been a great supporter of Willow's and assured her that he would help with Eli's recovery. Willow was surprised by the sight of her farm. The fields had been prepared for the spring planting season. All of the work had been done by the freed people from the Lumpkin's Jail that were now considered to be a part of Willow's family.

Harrison's body was returned to Cincinnati for burial at North Bend on Thursday, April 22, 1841, only three months after departing for Washington as president. Interred in the Ohio soil of the South Wind people, his tomb was built on the bones and spirits of the Shawnee.

CHAPTER 21

Trouble Comes in Pairs   September 1841   on the Ohio

September arrived with the blessing of a bumper harvest of crops. The harvest of medicine plants and roots was just as fruitful. Willow's new family from Lumpkin's Jail had built small homes on the land she had given them. The newly freed people had worked with vigor farming their land and making it more productive. They taught everyone who wanted to learn the gift of these southern farming techniques. Willow's farm was also made more productive by the knowledge of these people. They would all have extra crops to sell or give to the needful people of the region.

Willow was busy trying different remedies for Eli's recovery. He had not made much progress after having had numerous, massive seizures. This was a condition the Indians called the devil's dance. She thought about the potent poison she had made in Washington for the boost into hell for Harrison. Mayhap it would relieve Eli's pain for good. His death would allow him to pass into the Great Good Spirit world with his ancestors.

Willow knew she was close to childbirth. At forty-two summers old, a good blessing of the spirits would be needed to see her through. She was using the old Shawnee remedies to ensure the health of her baby. This medicine also helped her overall health, as she had not had any sickness for two months from the potent poison she was forced to drink.

Willow felt blessed that the poison that killed Harrison had not taken her or her baby's life. She also felt blessed to have the help of Genevieve, who had learned from Willow the art of midwifery. Knowing that her birthing time was near, Gen and Mother Washington (an old woman from the group of the freed people from Lumpkin's Jail) were staying at her home around the clock.

Mother Washington had become a great asset to Willow. She was always lending a helping hand with the birthing of the local population. With Mother's knowledge of ancient African medicines, Willow was given an opportunity to expand her worth as a healer.

Along with the other freed slaves, Mother Washington faced the old, antiquated 1807 Ohio slave laws. These laws caused significant hardships for all of these freed people. Each person was required to pay a $500 bond, which guaranteed their good behavior. Then they were required to obtain two signatures of white men on a voucher.

Under these same laws, blacks could not serve in the militias, attend white schools, or testify in court against white people. With Hiram's support, Willow helped pay their bonds. They also recruited local whites to obtain signatures for the vouchers to help keep these people free.

On Sunday, September 26, Willow awoke to severe pain. She knew her baby was coming into this world, so she woke Gen. Mother Washington was already up boiling water. It was as if she knew today would be the day. Willow's water broke at seven thirty in the morning.

The pain that Willow had experienced earlier that morning would only be a warning tickle compared with the pain that was yet to come. Willow had known much pain in her life, but nothing she had experienced had fully prepared her for this. She now knew firsthand the pain that birthing mothers had during her midwifery duties.

The birth went well, and at seven o'clock at night the delivery of a healthy baby boy entered this world of troubles. With her massive weight gain, he was smaller than Willow had expected. She had carried him for the full nine months. She believed conception had occurred on Christmas day. This would be her Christmas baby.

Hours had elapsed since the birth of David Thomas Reed, but the pain from the contractions was worse now than ever. Willow was concerned and afraid that she would die. She feared not being there for Eli and his new son.

She believed there may have been a residual effect from her own poison all those months ago that helped put Harrison in his grave.

Willow was back in the bed screaming with pain when Mother Washington said, "Yes! I see the problem, you are having baby number two!" Willow was giving birth to a brother for little David. At one o'clock in the morning, James Tecumseh Reed was born, just about six hours after David Thomas.

Willow's pain subsided as she cleaned James. She wrapped him in cloth and took both infants to Eli's room. At first, Eli remained expressionless. Then, as both babies began to cry in unison, a slight smile came to Eli's lips, and a solitary tear came to his eye. This was one of the happiest days of Willow's life.

Many days of joy passed from the birth of the twins into a Christmas season that should have been the best time of Willow's life. However, the slow progress of Eli's recovery dampened her joy. For a short while, Willow believed some progress was being made by the use of sign language with Eli. Now, more and more, she experienced failure in communicating.

On a cold December morning, with snow blowing and the winter wolf winds howling, Willow awoke to someone yelling from her back dooryard. Pete was there calling for her help. All she could understand was that it had something to do with Eli. Pete was pointing down the path that led to her barn. The blowing snow did not allow more than a glimpse of a dancing human figure.

As Willow approached, she could see that it was Eli. He was butt-naked with only his leather stump protector on his handless arm. Eli, with his head turned to the heavens, was chanting in his native Cherokee language. Along with his faithful dog Copper, he was dancing his heart out. Willow knew this was a good sign from the Great Good Spirit. She joined him and Copper in their dance.

CHAPTER 22

The Ghost of Willow Wood　　May 1964　　on the Ohio

The old, manual Reel Mower needed the blades sharpened. Parts were falling off of this backbreaking, man killer faster than I could put them back together. I was cutting Grandma Lu's lawn for the first time this year. It was late spring, and the lingering cold weather had slowed the growth of the spring elixir greens that Grandma Lu prized for her bowel clean-out.

Having to wait an extra two weeks to harvest her prized greens made the grass almost too tall for this mower. Grandma Lu's mood was worse than this raggedy mower's condition. *Oh man, here she comes! I am going to get the Lu version of how to use this raggedy, old mower.* Well, I went and did it! I made the mistake of saying, "I wish I were rich so I could buy you a good, power mower."

Grandma Lu looked at me with all the wisdom of her sixty-four years and said, "Wish in one hand and spit in the other, I bet you will not need to guess which one will fill up first." I had gotten little more than those types of nuggets of wisdom from my Grandma Lu during the past autumn and winter, and even less about Grandma Reed's story.

It didn't help matters any that President Kennedy was assassinated this past November. That tragic event caused Grandma Lu to clam up even more than she already had. She wanted the shame of what our family had done in 1841 to somehow vanish back into the closet with the other family skeletons.

I remember crying for two days when Kennedy was killed. What heartbreak that was for our country. *I wonder if anyone cried when Harrison died. I guess his family boohooed, and the other evil-doers waiting for his reign of power cried over their empty wallets.*

I finished mowing the lawn with Grandma Lu's nugget of wisdom floating around in my brain. My Mom and Web arrived in his old Packard to take us to Willow Wood. We were going on a family expedition to look for spring herbs, mushrooms, and grandma's coveted roots. I had never before gone to this place to hunt for roots and the other prized plants they loved.

Preparation for this hunt in the big woods always started with Grandma Lu's secret bug repellent oil. A good rubdown of this concoction repelled mosquitoes, ticks, gnats, and biting deer flies. I also believe the common cold would avoid you. Now I can't tell you what this stuff was made from, but the smell alone would repel most anything on this planet.

Heck, legend has it that this same anti-bug brew was used back in the day of the caveman Indians fifteen thousand years ago! The cave Indians had to battle such insects as the saber-toothed crotch crickets. Just think about one of those bad boys sinking a fang into you!

I had heard the story of Grandma Reed's death in these woods. Some locals believe her ghost still haunts these woods today. When the moon is in the right phase, you can see her collecting her crop of roots and herbs. They say not to look into her burn-scarred face, or you may be transformed into some forest animal like a squirrel, chipmunk or groundhog. *Dang! Why not a bear? That would be too cool to be a big old, mean bear.*

I was known to be as windy as a sack of farts, and this trip was no different. I couldn't leave well enough alone, I had to ask questions about this legend to get my imagination juiced up. I had been told for many years that I was born under the veil. That meant having soothsayer abilities, seeing into the future, seeing dead people, telling your fortune, and all that other junk.

It seemed like my family always worked overtime to fill my head full of stuff. I think they only started saying that to scare me and keep me from running the streets at night. It didn't work, though. I ran the streets anyway.

I settled into a good routine of finding plants and showing them to

Mom or Grandma Lu for their approval to harvest as they wanted to also protect different species from over-harvesting. Some of the ancient medicine plants no longer existed in these woods, maybe not even in this world. Some have been gone for over one hundred years. *Wow! A fly made a glider path landing onto my bug oil-soaked arm. Jeez! The darn thing just died there before it could take off!*

After having drifted into a deep ravine, I looked back up the hill through the thin, spring foliage and saw the root-gathering group at the crest of the ridge. I thought I could find a good place to be lazy for a short while. Instead, I found a beautiful grove of sassafras and knew this was an important find, as it is one of the ingredients for the making of kinnikinnick.

I looked up the ridge, nobody was in sight. Now at this point, my imagination started to kick into high gear. What little sun that had filtered through was now blocked by a cloud, which made the woods darker than when I was with the group. With some relief, I thought I could hear them calling me from the ridge to my right. I began to walk in that direction.

To my amazement, I caught a strong whiff of kinnikinnick smoke. As I rounded a large hickory tree, I was surprised to see an old lady digging roots. *I thought we had these woods to our lonesome, free for the picking!*

The old lady slowly got to her feet. She wore a buckskin dress that hung down to her ankles. I had never seen a picture of my Grandma Ciicothe Reed. But I guess if they had cameras to take pictures during the 1800's, our family couldn't have afforded one anyway. From the stories I was told and the description I had in my mind's eye of her, the woman with the burned face and damaged eye in front of me would be that image.

A calmness came over me like I never knew. The image began metamorphosing before my eyes from an old woman into a young lady. With half of her face covered with burn scars, she was still an unbelievably beautiful woman. She extended her hand; in it was a blood-red root. I accepted her offering. In a quiet, musical voice, she said, "Remember the stories of the people and protect the secrets of the tomb." Then she turned and quickly walked away, fading from my sight, leaving only a pleasant scent in the air.

I didn't know what to do, wind my head or scratch my watch. My brain was spinning, but I was not afraid. *At least I wasn't turned into a chipmunk with nuts in my cheek pouches.* I stared at the root in my hand. I always had trouble accepting gifts from heaven, or so my dad claimed.

One example is from when we lived in Union Landing, Ohio. An 18 wheeler rig that was hauling a truckload of hogs for delivery to the meat processing plant in Gallipolis, Ohio delivered a gift from heaven to the Johnson family instead. The railroad underpass on old US Hwy 52 was flooded from the heavy rains of that morning. The rig got stuck in the high water. To keep the hogs in the lower tier of the truck from drowning, the driver opened the tailgate and the race was on!

My pops rounded the empty hog lot and ran into the barnyard screaming as if he had gone nuts! He was yelling for me and my brother Mike to get our asses in gear as there were hogs from heaven. Yes! All around us was a gift from God in the cornfields that surrounded the property; hogs, hogs, and more hogs!

Now daddy, having made his living as a big rig driver, had a degree of compassion for this driver, who was offering two dollars for each live hog returned. Not only did we end the day with twelve pigs in our once empty lot, but the old man also had a pocket full of money to go out drinking that night. This was accomplished by our work of returning fourteen hogs, all but one, alive.

We ate the dead, fat hog that night with the driver's blessing. Our just reward for our effort was to get our behinds back into the cornfield and help our neighbor harvest some of his corn. I guess this field corn could also be a gift from heaven.

I was snapped out of my thoughts about the gifts from above by a familiar voice screeching my name. Just like magic, I saw Grandma Lu coming down the hill. She looked ticked off. Screaming in an angry tone, she asked "Where the hell have you been? Didn't you hear us calling your name?"

When she saw the root I was holding, everything changed. I told her about finding the grove of sassafras. Then seeing the burn-scarred, old woman. Nothing seemed to get her attention until I described how the woman gave me this particular root.

Grandma Lu did not appear surprised at the mention of the old lady, as if it were an everyday occurrence to see a ghost in these woods. Instead, she stood there slack-jawed looking at this root as though she was looking at gold. She may have believed it was gold because she had not seen the Indian death bloodroot for years.

The spring daylight had turned to dusk. Grandma Lu had worked like a beaver to hide the location of her precious root patch. She was most likely praying that no other root hunters would find it. She also worked with loving care not to disturb the plants that she believed may be the last of their kind on this side of heaven.

Grandma Lu seemed nervous during the ride home. She did not want me to talk about my encounter with Grandma Reed's ghost. As always, I didn't know when to keep my mouth shut; the diarrhea of the mouth started to flow. I was shocked when Grandma Lu back-handed me across the lips. Needless to say, that buttoned up my mouth real quick.

CHAPTER 23

The Protector of the Bones   September 1964   Ironton on the Ohio

The blasting, the large equipment, and the earth movers all seemed to materialize overnight. But in reality, the work on the expansion of US Hwy 52 along the rim of hills behind Ironton, Ohio had been going on for years. The old route of US Hwy 52 followed Second and Third Streets, which were the main streets through Ironton. There was a danger of big rigs or heavy traffic coming through the main drag of town, and you had to dart or run like a chicken with its flipping head cut off to avoid getting run down when crossing the street.

The new highway would be a positive change for our community, or so that's what the big wigs told us. The realization hit me like a ton of the rocks that the road crew was blasting. If they were expanding US Hwy 52 behind Ironton, they were most likely doing the same within the hills behind South Point. Tecumseh's tomb would be right in their path. A sickening pain hit my gut, and I upchucked my skimpy lunch all over my raggedy converse shoes.

Magoo and I had prowled the Indian hills behind Ironton more times than I could count searching for artifacts, arrowheads, and spear points. We walked the trails and climbed the cliffs, enjoying the views of the Ohio River from these pristine hills. Now the gentle sloping hills that trailed into Ironton had been blasted.

The blasting had cut a sheer rock face of five hundred feet. Giant rocks with Indian hieroglyphs were blasted into a thousand pieces. An untold number of Indian bones would soon have traffic running on top of them. I had to do something to save the bones in the tomb of Tecumseh! My plan was simple; I had no flipping plan!

My main man Magoo and I hauled ass on Saturday, only a few days before my birthday and the date my Grandma Wick died this past year. I think she would be proud of me for making an effort to protect the secret tomb. During the past year, I had my doubts about the story I was told. However, the trip to Willow Wood and the encounter with Grandma Reed's ghost in the late spring changed that. I had bad dreams every night. Maybe I had too much of a radical imagination, but this story was becoming all too real to me.

I was not ready for what we saw as we neared the section of road construction where I thought we might find the skull-shaped boulder. The rock was now at the top of a stair-step cut cliff face five hundred feet in the sky. All I could do was stand and look into the air like I had been struck by lightning with my hair on fire. Magoo finally snapped me out of my stupor by telling me to wake up.

As I looked up, I saw a state highway pickup truck speeding towards us. There was no getting away. Before we could jump onto our raggedy bikes, the road boss was on us like stink on a dog's turd. He skidded the truck to a dusty stop; the door flew open. He was practically out of the truck before it completely stopped. He moved awful fast for a fat boy, and was in our grills before you could say, "Boo."

The road boss was only inches from my face, close enough that I could smell the Kentucky Apple plug chewing tobacco on his hot breath. He was ticked and told us that we were within three hundred yards of a blast zone and that when the siren sounded, we would be three minutes from an explosion of rock that would land all over the exact spot where were standing, burying us. I looked him in the eye and said, "This is my Grandma Lu's property, and you are the trespassers, not us."

He laughed for a minute, then told us, "All of this land has either been condemned or purchased by the state for the expansion of the road. If you or your GRANNY LU have a problem with that, take it up with Governor

Rhodes." Then he laughed again. As he turned, he kicked Magoo in the rear and said, "Get the hell out of here before I call the police."

Magoo and I were bummed out. We looked at the rock tomb in the sky from a safe distance on US Hwy 52. We wondered if it was next to come crashing down. *Would the bones of the Great Chief Tecumseh, Uncle Yellow Robe, and my other ancestors go flying through the air like they had wings, only to become a part of the highway foundation?*

As we rode about a mile back in the direction of the Ashland Bridge, we saw a low-cut valley that would allow us to hide our bikes. We hoped this would give us an easy climb parallel with the steep-cut ridge, and that it could possibly be a way to the rock tomb. The climb was harder than we thought. After Magoo had scared us by slipping on the edge of the five-hundred-foot drop and grabbing onto a small tree, we came upon the base of the giant boulder.

The tomb was further back from the sheared rock face than it appeared from the new roadbed. There was some relief that it was in no immediate danger of coming down. The thick tangle of briars was still at the base creating an impenetrable barrier into the boulder unless you knew the angle of the entrance.

Magoo and I ran through the briars like two wild rabbits. Magoo had more trouble than I did due to his six-foot frame. We started the climb up the rock face. Magoo led the way. I was behind him telling him what he needed to do. He made it look easy because the hand and footholds were cut for a man of his size, not for a runt like me.

As I topped the rock face where it turned out, a blast boomed in the distance. My feet came out of the holes, and I was hanging on by my fingernails! When I saw Magoo's big, black hand come over the rim and grab onto my skinny wrist, I knew why I had the premonition to bring him to this sacred place. He pulled me onto the top of the stone tomb like a rag doll.

We both lay there breathing hard. I knew that I had cheated death for the second time in a little over a year. Magoo was there both times to pull my biscuits out of the fire. At last, I caught my breath enough to tell him thanks and to let him know that I was glad he was my blood brother.

As always when I made that claim, Magoo smiled a toothy grin and said, "Blood brothers from different mothers forever," and he gripped my hand.

When we got on our feet and saw the carvings on the top of this stone, I knew this was the right rock. We could not believe the panoramic view of the Ohio River. Much of the virgin timber that had blocked the view before had been cut down for the new road construction.

After we had taken in the scenery, we turned our attention to the chimney hole opening on the back side of the boulder. The hole was gone; all that remained was a seam with a wide fissure at the place where the chimney hole once existed. I could only imagine what had gone on in the tomb; maybe the entire thing had collapsed. There was one thing for sure, no one could go in from the top!

I know Magoo must not believe me about there being a chimney opening. But I remember the fresh airflow that came through that hole when I fell down it during my first visit. As I recovered the rope to get out, air had hit my face from inside the tomb. *Maybe there was an alternate cave opening at the base!* We scoured the forest floor like two squirrels looking for nuts. As we cleared away the dried leaves, we hoped to find another opening to the tomb.

I was on the verge of giving up when Magoo gave out a scream like a mashed cat. Thinking he had gotten hurt, I ran to where he was. When I got there, he was shoulder deep into a cave opening with his rear sticking up in the air. The opening was fifty feet from the base of the great stone. While backing out, Magoo said that the opening was too small, even for a skinny guy like me. But if you know anything about me, I was going to give it a try anyway.

We had brought our flashlights with us. Magoo's light was a little better than mine. After going in only ten feet, I got stuck. Thank God for Magoo! He pulled me free just as I began to panic.

I retrieved the small hatchet we had brought, thinking I could cut some large roots at the narrow opening. *Maybe we could make the entrance wide enough for my melon-sized head.* The tree roots were an easy cut. The removal of the roots, as well as some soil and small rocks, made the opening wide enough to pass into the larger tunnel.

I prayed not to come face to face with an animal. I thought that this was maybe a bear's cave. *If Mr. Bear were in here getting ready for a winter's nap and only needed one last snack before bedtime, it would be ME!*

The tunnel opening was wide, allowing me to crawl. The entire time I was in there, Magoo called out to me for reassurance that I was still alive. I crawled on my hands and knees for what seemed like fifty feet. I finally came to an area where I could stand up.

In front of me was a wall of roots, most likely from the giant hickory and buckeye trees next to the monolithic stone above. They looked like a door or curtain blocking, no guarding, the entrance to a large room or cavern. As I started to cut the roots with the hatchet, an old, musty odor hit me in the face.

I had finally cleared enough of the roots to enter the large cave. The roof was ten feet high and appeared to have been manmade. I thought this was the small tomb I went into from the chimney hole at the top of the rock before, but it was not. This was a different tomb.

The walls had carved platforms of stone that served as beds for the skeletons. The skulls lay facing the east, the feet pointed towards the west. All of them were covered with some type of tree bark. I began counting, and at thirty sets of bones, I was interrupted by a faint voice echoing through the opening of the tunnel. I went to the opening and called out to Magoo. Hearing that I was still alive and kicking, his response sounded as if he had calmed down some.

Turning my attention back to the tomb, I knew I needed to hurry. Magoo's old flashlight was dying out fast, and I knew mine was not much of a backup; I had to move quickly. I worked my way to what I thought was the back of the cave when I saw a skeleton. It was adorned with what seemed like paint, feathers, and a special tomahawk carved at the handle in the grip of its bony hand. There was a long-stemmed, stone, smoking pipe pinched between its teeth. Two skeletons were sitting on the floor at the base of the platform as if they had sat down there and died.

I tripped over a large medicine bag laying at their bony feet. The rattle of the bones forced me to take a closer look. There were animal bones among the foot bones that I had scattered across the cave floor. *These must be old Copper's bones! He must have found this cave entrance long before Magoo and I stumbled into it. One thing's for sure, you don't have to be a brain surgeon to figure out that this was the Great Chief Tecumseh!*

I found a small opening in a space between the burial platforms. It appeared to have been made by a type of mud and stone that had the look of the natural stone walls. Along the entire length of the false wall were scratch marks. *Copper must have tried his best to get into the chamber with his master.*

The removal of the false wall went quickly with the use of the hatchet. I climbed up an incline of hand and footholds to an air hole. This wall was constructed of the same material as the false wall below. I broke through the wall to find the smaller tomb that held the bones of Uncle Yellow Robe, Elijah Dials and of someone that I had thought was Tecumseh on my first visit.

Now I knew for a fact that my Grandma Ciicothe Reed did not find the actual tomb of Tecumseh. What she believed to be Tecumseh's tomb was, in fact, a decoy. I could see the empty Cold Wave soda pop bottle next to what should have been a petrified bologna sandwich. It was gone, eaten by God knows what.

I began to panic. The opening to the chimney hole had collapsed in on itself. It had a stress crack running along the overhead, but everything looked stable up above. I said a quick prayer and returned down the shaft into the larger tomb. I placed the items belonging to Grandma Wick on Tecumseh's burial platform with hopes of removing the curse of bad dreams from my mind.

I quickly headed for the exit tunnel as a humongous blast went off. The bones jumped into the air; some fell from the burial platforms. I fell to the tomb's floor as a small stone fell, giving me a glancing blow to the left side of my head. Ancient tomb dust boiled up blinding the weak light of Magoo's flashlight. My vision was fading, and my brain was spinning.

Grandma Wick's voice was as clear as if we were sitting in the old shotgun house on Ninth and Pine Streets. In a low, whimsical voice, she told me more of her stories. She asked me to remember the curse of Tecumseh. She said that this is the year the earth would shake and open.

The dust cleared as my brain did the same. I was lying face to face with Copper's skull. I was close enough that if he had lips, he could have kissed me. Desperate and trembling, I found the flashlight. I knew my good luck was running thin and that I must get out!

As I entered the exit tunnel, I could hear Magoo screaming at the top of his lungs. Dust remained suspended in the air through the full length of the shaft. When I arrived at the most narrow place in the tunnel, I had a head-on collision with Magoo, who was stuck trying to come to my rescue.

I thought about how much I loved this big knucklehead but did not want to end my life looking into the eyes of this wild man. Maybe if he died first I could eat him, then the tunnel would be clear, and I would be home free. Magoo was not in favor of that plan, so I pushed as he walked crawdad-like backwards. After what seemed like an hour or more we were free, just in time for the next US Hwy 52 blast in the distance!

At first, I thought the dust coming from the mouth of the tomb tunnel entrance was bad news. But after thinking about it, I came to the conclusion that blocking the only entrance was a good thing. As the dust cleared, I could look into the tunnel opening. I saw that the narrow space was almost entirely closed. Magoo and I gathered rocks, finished blocking off the opening, then added dried brush. We felt sure in our hearts that we had done all that we could to protect the tomb's secrets. *We ARE the bone protectors!*

We headed for the section of South Point where Magoo's aunt lives. I couldn't get the thought of Grandma Wick's voice ringing in my head, warning me to remember the curse of Tecumseh. *What does it mean?* I had been told about the earthquakes that were said to have been predicted by Tecumseh in 1811-1812, and the quake that damaged the town of Anna, Ohio. The old people told us there would be a curse of earthquakes on a fifty-year cycle. If that was true, the next great earthquake was not too far in the future.

I pedaled my bike as fast as I could to keep up with Magoo. The strange pulsing of Eli's pawaka stone in my pocket startled me back to reality. This was especially stressing because I knew that I had put it back in the tomb.

My thoughts drifted back to the present as we arrived at the home of Magoo's aunt. His family always treated me as if I were a part of their family. His aunt had lived on this farm all her life. Her family had inherited this land from her father, whose family had owned it for over one hundred years. The road construction had taken a large tract of it towards the hills. When I told her that my Grandma Ciicothe Reed had owned land near this property, her face became drawn. Her eyes focused on me like she could not understand my words.

I thought I had heard all of the fantastic stories about my Grandma Reed's lifetime. At times, I had my doubts about the truth spun into these legends. What I heard from Magoo's aunt reinforced what I had been told by my Grandmas Wick and Lu. Somehow I was not surprised to learn that her great-great-grandmother was rescued in Virginia around 1841 by my great-great-great-grandmother Ciicothe Reed.

I was shocked that his aunt believed that she was some distant kin to William Henry Harrison, the slave master that was killed by Grandma Reed. *Magoo's great-great-great-grandma must have been the young girl rescued from the Lumpkin's Jail slavers! Some bones need to remain buried, never to be protected.* I headed home with Eli's stone in my pocket. I had no clue as to how it had materialized back into my raggedy dungarees. I prayed that it would not explode before I could get home.

CHAPTER 24

Will the Last Indian to Depart Ohio Turn off the Lights
1843   Cincinnati on the Ohio

The twins, or The Brothers Reed as everyone called them, were not quite two years old. They had gained a reputation as the meanest two-year-olds along this stretch of the Ohio. Willow always told people that her boys were full of piss and vinegar.

Eli was showing marked signs of improvement each day. He had fewer convulsions and was able to communicate on a limited basis. Eli had a partial paralysis of the left side. He joked that at least he had no hand on that side to worry about losing control of. He was able to work at the David's store and help spoil his boys at home. Eli's midnight dancing slowed to an occasional naked foray in the back dooryard or an uncontrolled howling at the moon.

On August 1, 1843, Willow traveled by wagon to Cincinnati to meet William Merrell. Her friend William could help market her remedies made from native medicines. She also wanted to show him some of her finds of the roots that she had thought to be extinct. The freed slaves had done an impressive job at finding these plants. Their love of the environment was equal to her own.

While in Cincinnati, Willow learned about the arrival of the Wyandot Tribe. The Wyandot were the last Indians in Ohio to have their lands stripped from them. After their removal from the state, the only Indians that remained were at hideouts like Willow's. The Removal Act, empowered by Jackson's belief that the only good Indian is a dead Indian, made the Ohio Whig's last land grab possible.

Chief Jacques of the Wyandot, met with Willow. He told her about his great sadness of having to leave their homelands. He described a good visit that he had with the Great White Father of Ohio at Columbus while on their journey south. Governor Wilson Shannon assured Chief Jacques that a beautiful plaque would be placed at Sandusky to mark the place where the Wyandot people once lived.

The information did not make the pain in his heart go away, nor did his people's anguish disappear. His tribe's land had already been reduced to 109,000 acres near Sandusky. There had been no hostility between the white people and the Wyandot for nearly fifty years, since the signing of the treaty at Greenville with old Blacksnake, General Wayne. Chief Jacques was proud to say that many of the remaining seven hundred tribe members had converted to Christianity. None of this made a difference to the white man with their overwhelming greed for land.

Willow told Chief Jacques that she was born on the Maumee River shortly after the Treaty of Greenville was signed. This sacred document did not stop them from moving her people to Prophetstown on the Tippecanoe. The white man never respected any of their papers. They were only used as paper to wipe their behinds, just like the other treaties signed with the Shawnee and other tribes.

Willow asked Chief Jacques if he knew the whereabouts of her Shawnee people, and whether or not any survived. He could not give her any good news. He thought the entire tribe had been massacred, and that she might be the last Shawnee on this earth.

Chief Jacques described the horror that occurred on the day his tribe arrived at the port of Cincinnati. A soldier lost his mind and killed a blue hair that was in a prayer circle. This caused the chief's people to refuse to board the great canoe. Some braves looked for weapons to use, not wanting to turn the other cheek. The governor had sent a counselor to calm the situation.

The Wyandot people had to go say goodbye to their beloved Ohio and their ancestors' bones. Willow thought that an additional plaque that said, "Here lies the last Indian killed in Ohio" should be placed at the port of Cincinnati for the murdered blue hair.

Willow made the short trip to North Bend wanting only to pray at the gravesite of Morning Star. She knew this was a huge risk as a reward was on her head. The reward was to be paid by the Harrison family for her capture and return as a slave.

Willow easily made it to the gravesite where Morning Star's ashes were buried. She fell to her knees and began to pray. While deep in prayer, she asked God to forgive her of her transgressions and her inabilities to save her loved ones. She was startled back to reality by a familiar voice from her past. Willow turned and looked into the watery eyes of old George, who had whispered her name. He had tears of joy from seeing her.

George explained that the Harrison family had reported Ciicothe dead, at least that was the rumor that was running its course through the slave community. They discussed the Harrison family's belief that Ciicothe had poisoned the old general, causing his death. They chose not to make this information public. This was just another of a long list of old family secrets. Willow was not sure about the Harrisons' reasoning. She assumed it had something to do with the old general's letters as well as their prideful way of thinking.

Willow and old George had a tearful goodbye. He explained that he could not come to her home at South Point as this would most likely lead the Harrison family to her location. He also said that if they had the God-given chance to meet again, he would share some dark Harrison family secrets that he sadly carried close to the vest.

As Willow returned to South Point with her family, she pondered the conversations that she had on her journey to Cincinnati and the evil that always lurks in the darkness. On the Ohio, everyone was working hard to secure the harvest for the upcoming winter. She had visited with Reverend Rankin on the return trip, who talked about their continued abolitionist efforts and the developing rumblings of a civil war.

On her first night back, Willow dreamed about the good South Wind people. *The world could have been so different.* She vowed to protect her two boys, their blood, and the blood of Tecumseh with her life.

During the end of the harvest moon in October, Willow's world started crashing down around her. Eli had been gone for three days when he returned from a drunken stupor. He had always avoided the white man's whiskey in the past. Willow believed the head wound he received in Washington had changed that.

Eli had started hearing voices. He told everyone that the chatter in his head never ended. At first, the chatter had no meaning or purpose. Then it developed into a maddening scramble of voices telling him what to do. Even with the news about Willow's possible pregnancy, she couldn't pull Eli out of this malaise, nor the slow spin into his own personal hell.

On a cold December morning, Willow awoke to the sound of footfalls on her back dooryard porch. Copper was howling like a wounded wolf. She had fallen asleep in her kitchen waiting for Eli to return from a night of drinking at the Frog Town saloons.

Willow could hear the urgency in the voices outside. She knew something bad had happened. Within the past two months, Willow had patched Eli's broken body more times than she would like to remember. She hurried to the door, grabbing her medicine tote on the way. Willow knew there would be the same need on this night.

CHAPTER 25

In the Tears of God   1843-1844   South Point on the Ohio

Willow could see that the return of her drunkard Cherokee was different this time. There was a group in a frenzy already gathering on her back porch. Behind them, her panic-stricken neighbors carried Eli's lifeless body. As soon as Willow touched his face, she knew he was not in this life. Eli had gone to the Great Good Spirit's world. Willow was three months pregnant. She would have to raise this unborn baby, along with the twins, by herself. She felt completely alone.

Willow's neighbors explained how they found Eli hanging by the neck from a large branch of the ancient buckeye tree on the old river road three miles west of her home. They handed her a note that had been stuck to Eli's chest with his own hunting knife. The note was blood stained, but Willow could make out the two words: NOT DONE.

Stuffed into Eli's mouth was a buckeye nut, or, as the Indians knew it, the Hetuck (meaning the eye of the buck). A cold chill ran the length of her spine. This was a bad Shawnee omen. Willow had been wrong in thinking that the last Indian had been killed in Cincinnati.

Willow did not know who to blame for Eli's murder, as there was plenty of hate to go around. She could only speculate that the Harrison family was involved. Mayhap it was the long-knife haters of the Indian people, or possibly the southern abolitionist haters. The Indians who remained in Ohio and tried to assimilate into the white society as she had done, were being tracked down by death mongers who showed no mercy.

While reflecting on Eli's death, she remembered about the Wilson family. The kin of the two brothers that he had killed during his murderous run to Kentucky would surely want him dead. Mayhap there were a hundred more enemies. She could only guess.

Willow busied herself with the preparations for a Christian funeral service for her beloved Eli. The private burial at the tomb of Tecumseh would take place later. Eli's body lay in repose in the living room as was the custom of these days. Friends coming from a long distance would have a chance to pay their last respects. However, Willow believed they had more enemies that would want to come and piss on Eli's bones rather than pray for him.

Nightmares invaded Willow's mind that night after the Christian service. Eli was the first to visit. He stood beside her bed. He was gory and in a partially decomposed state. His putrefied breath blew cold in her face. Willow felt her body levitate from the bed. She was in panic within her own nightmare. She felt as if her heart would explode.

Willow awoke as she crashed to the floor. Eli's words echoed in her head. Now at least she had some idea about his last day on this side of the circle of time. If she believed in the dead talking beyond the grave, she knew who had killed him. At least Willow had enough information to cover her back.

The horror for Willow was the who. She needed to be cautious. Yes, it was only a dream. But it held a warning she needed to heed: keep your friends close, but your enemies closer.

The interment at the tomb of Tecumseh went well. The weather had turned mild for the season, which was a blessing. Copper remained at the tomb with a forlorn look on his face. Willow had never seen this look before, on man nor beast.

Willow's nightmares continued, climaxing with an awe-inspiring conversation with God. This meeting with God seemed to occur during the summer month of July, one day before the celebration of the revolution for the freedom from the king of England. God was sitting in a handmade, cane rocking chair that looked a lot like the one that Eli made for her the previous summer.

God looked upset. A solitary tear was dripping from his right eye. Contained in God's tear was the entire universe. She somehow knew without asking that it would take one million years for this tear to fall. The South Wind people were all sitting with Willow at the base of this huge chair, yet somehow they were not small or insignificant in God's eyes.

At first glance, God appeared to be a man. At second glance, God was a woman. God had no need to speak, and the people did not have to hear. All of the talking took place through their hearts and minds. God expressed his great displeasure at the white man's greed: the killing, theft of the lands, and breaking the laws with no regard for the Good Book's lessons. God's hand moved towards the falling tear.

Without speaking Willow knew God's intent was to destroy the universe, it had gotten too evil. Willow did not know how she had become the spokesperson for humankind, yet she was. Someone must have died, which put her in this position. Communicating with God, representing all mankind, was a daunting task. She would do her best.

Willow could see God's hand within an inch of the teardrop. If hit, the tear and the universe would be destroyed. She was not sure how she knew that one inch equaled about five hundred billion light-years in distance. Nor was she sure of the meaning of a light-year, but she knew it had to be a great distance.

The case Willow made for God to give humankind a second chance was good. Just as she was receiving his agreement for a hundred years of peace, her water broke. Willow awoke from this most pleasant dream to the fact that a new life was coming into this world, a world she had somehow saved from sure destruction.

On July 4, 1844, Willow brought a baby girl into a world full of turmoil. She knew she would have to work hard to protect this child. Willow was not sure how much of her life remained on this side of the circle of time. She was positive of one thing: she would give that life to protect her children, they were what she lived for.

Willow knew from her dreams that God was displeased with her revenge killing of the evil man Harrison. Vengeance is God's sole responsibility. It was not intended for use by the human race. She understood this concept yet still had revenge in her heart for Eli's murderers.

Willow was certain the world had been spared for a short time in God's eye. *Could mankind change?* Willow did not think that they could nor want to change. The greed would control their lives, as greed was the root of all evil in this life. It was the cause of all wars, addictions, and cruelty in this world. She could not change what God could not change.

Willow's baby girl was the spitting image of Blue Turtle Eyes (Mary), who was born years ago on the Great Miami. Willow knew this was another sign from God. What meaning it held, she had no idea at this time. She must live and see what God has in store for her. In her heart, she knew these words from the Good Book: "The wrath of man does not accomplish the righteousness of God." Willow prayed for strength to live by the words of her Bible.

Willow was comfortable sitting in the cane chair made for her by Eli. She was nursing her new baby girl. She had named her "Alaque," the Shawnee name for Star. Willow loved her baby's bright, star-filled, blue eyes.

The summer heat had been oppressive during the month of July. She could see a man approaching in the distance. Dressed in black, heavyweight, winter clothing, he had the appearance of the white man's undertaker. Willow gripped her trusted tomahawk, ready to use it if need be.

The stranger removed his top hat and leaned heavily on a skull-head cane. He introduced himself as Mordecai Smith and spoke in a voice with a haunting rasp from hell. He said, "Ciicothe, I have made a long journey with news from your beloved, the newly departed Eli." Willow, with her jaw slack, just sat there trembling as the tomahawk pulsed in her hand. *How did he know my Shawnee name? And who is this mysterious man?*

To Willow, the journey to the David and Sons General Store seemed to take hours. The twins were in the flatbed of the wagon fighting tooth and nail while little Alaque was in Willow's papoose fussing up a storm. The strange man Mordecai, who was sitting on the buckboard, continued talking. Most of what he said did not make good, common sense for Willow to comprehend.

Mordecai had revealed his troubled nightmares about these nightly visits of Eli Dials to Willow. He had described her beloved Cherokee in every detail, which sent chills down her spine. He told her about the ghost's demands for Willow to ask Hiram for that which was lost. She would soon have the answer.

Hiram was not surprised by Willow's request nor by the odd story about the ghost communicating with the crazy-looking Mordecai. He had almost forgotten about the box that had been stored at his business for more than twenty years. Hiram led the way through the narrow storage area, all the while keeping a jaded eye on this strange man Mordecai Smith. Hiram found the rough-hewn, wooden box and removed the boxes that were stacked on top of it. It was now his turn to surprise Willow. He drew the group in close to begin the story of the mysterious box.

The box first appeared in Uncle Yellow Robe's property that was recovered by Hiram a short time after he had saved Willow's beloved uncle from the hangman's rope. Uncle Yellow Robe had lived with Hiram for two years when on a cold, December morning he came to Hiram's cabin with the box asking him to protect it. He said that someday, someone in great need would seek that which was lost. Hiram said, "I do not know the contents. On numerous occasions, I was tempted to open it, but I kept my promise not to."

The group had returned to the main store. Willow was ready to open the box. She had declined Hiram's offer of privacy. The leather hinges resisted as they had petrified over the many years of storage. While trying to open the box, the hinges broke, and the lid came off completely. A musty mist of dust swirled into the air like a ghost that had long been entombed within. Willow looked in to see a small part of an ancient white buffalo hide, the same type used in wrapping the sacred Shawnee bundle.

The commotion at the pickle barrel distracted Willow. The twins were fighting over a half-eaten cucumber pickle. One threatening, hairy eyeball look from Willow was enough to calm the ruckus. She returned to the task of slowly opening the white bison hide.

As Willow looked at the objects inside, her jaw dropped open. She turned to look at Hiram and Mordecai, their jaws were also slack. Their eyes were set on the contents of the box. Willow had seen the roughly carved figures before at Prophetstown during the Christmas season.

The Nativity was one of her uncle's most prized belongings. He brought it with him from his life at Gnadenhutten on the Tuscarawas. They had been carved by the Reverend Zeisberger in Schoenbrunn. She remembered the prayers of thanks to the child in the manger during the Christmas season of hope.

The only other belonging in the hide wrapping was her uncle's carved, wooden crucifix. It was now clear what old Thomas (Uncle Yellow Robe) was trying to say. What was lost was her walk through life with the man Jesus. A man, the son of God who gave his life to save hers, a concept she had lost. From the grave, old Thomas was trying to remind her how to live on this side of the circle of life.

Willow sat relaxing on her back dooryard porch. She looked into the distance as the silhouette of Mordecai Smith vanished down the Ohio River road. Before leaving, he had a hearty breakfast with her, all the while describing his premonitions of the Great War to come and how this war could take her boys on a perilous journey. Willow would have ignored his rambling comments, but was cautious not to take him lightly after the events of the past two days.

Willow's thoughts drifted to the legends told around the fire pits at Prophetstown, and of how the man Jesus walked with the South Wind people long before the white man had arrived in this land. Jesus was known as the man of a thousand tongues. He was a man that walked the wilderness unharmed, a man of peace and love. Willow now knew the course she must take in this life, not only for her good but for the welfare of her children.

CHAPTER 26

Grandma Lu Goes Old School Prophet   November 1964   Ironton on the Ohio

Roots, roots, and more roots! I saw flipping roots in my dreams! We hunted these God-blessed haunted woods for that Shawnee, blood-sucking root until I was blue in the face! The small patch of rootstock that Grandma Reed's ghost directed me to was not enough to wet Grandma Lu's whistle.

Heck yeah, I was ticked! I could have been running the streets with my road dogs Magoo and Castle. But no, I was forced into "Shank's Pony" (the name my Grandma Lu used to describe Web's old car, the big, black Packard Clipper). I am not sure why she called it that, but I bet it's over my head and beyond my years.

Today my brother Bubby was helping. When he put his heart into root hunting, he could tear up the woods! With the cold November weather and an early freeze, plants were hard to identify so root finding could be scarce. I think Grandma Lu wanted me to cohort with the ghost in the woods. That would help find the exact location of the bloodroot.

Dang it! I don't feel like root hunting today. In fact, I don't know why this rootstock is so important to my grandma. You may have learned by now that I don't know when to keep my big mouth shut. I had to ask my Grandma Lu, "Just what good are these bloodroots anyway?"

I could see an anger in her eyes that I had never seen before. Maybe it was the one year anniversary of the assassination of our President Kennedy that had her grackle up. Maybe it was my loose lips. I could only guess. There was one thing for sure, I needed to shut my mouth and listen.

Grandma Lu was right on the verge of jacking my jaw. She knew I had failed to see the greater picture of the stories that I had been privileged to hear. One being the revelation that my Indian kinfolk were involved in the poisoning of a president. Another from the trips I took to the ancient tomb of Tecumseh. No, my eyes were still closed to the real meaning of all this.

I could only guess that I was in training to be the next family Shaman, the Maykujay medicine man, and healer. But most importantly, to be the protector of our family secrets. The Great Good Spirit God had a mission for my dumb ass, and I had not fully opened my eyes to what that mission was. Maybe I would soon wake up and get a clue as to what I must do to embrace this honor.

I looked up just in the nick of time to see Grandma Lu rushing in my direction with her coat flapping in the wind. She was obviously pissed and was preparing to put a haymaker on my jaw. I was standing on an outcropping of rock that had a five-foot drop into a shallow ravine.

My next move was graceful, it had me tripping over my own feet and falling into the gully. As always, I lucked out by breaking my fall with my hard head on some moss-covered rocks. I was laying on my side looking up into the seething eyes of my Grandma Lu. Yep, I was shaking like a dog shitting razor blades. I was thankful that the only thing badly hurt was my pride.

Grandma Lu maneuvered down to my location like a mountain goat. She did not lose her footing one time. *The agility that she has at her age always impresses me.* Bending forward, she roughly helped me to my feet. She told me that I had a lot to learn in this life.

With a look of shock on her face, Grandma Lu's eyes focused well beyond me to a spot ten feet up the other side of the ravine. All she could say was, "There it is." She dropped me like a sack of spuds, and ran towards the object that had taken me out of the limelight. I knew it might not last for long, so I needed to pull my act together.

As I approached the object of Grandma Lu's attention, I could see that it was a plant that was not in my repertoire of herbal medicines. Grandma Lu was down on her knees as if she was praying. All the old woman could say was, "Thank the Lord," over and over again. *Maybe now I am off the hook from getting my butt kicked.* She turned in my direction and motioned for me to come over.

I stood with her over this sacred find. My Grandma Lu explained the great importance of this plant's medicinal value. She described how it was used to save lives during the Civil War. It maybe even helped the North to win. To say I was slack-jawed and surprised could not express my real feelings.

I thought of only wanting to learn a little history about our family's Indian heritage over the past two summers. This all started with my pit-jumping stupidity. And, it became a journey of one shocking revelation after another.

With all this information overload, I have learned from my Grandma Lu that I have only skimmed the surface of the stories and legends concerning my Grandma Ciicothe Reed. I know now that history is the result of what the writer wants to make of it, and by putting down on paper what he or she wants the reader to believe. The Indians' history is told by passing down their stories from generation to generation by the people who lived them.

I awoke that night in a cold sweat, with nightmares haunting my sleep. They were most likely the result of the tidbits of stories that Grandma Lu had imparted during our return trip from Willow Wood. It could be caused by Eli's crystal clear pawaka stone that I had removed from the tomb of Tecumseh and brought home with me. *Did that make me a grave robber like the thousands of white men who claim to be preserving history by taking artifacts from the Indian graves? What is my next step, grave robbing in Woodland Cemetery?* Some things are better left buried!

I had a tough week after our trip to Willow Wood. Everything should have been great after the discovery of Grandma Lu's prized roots. The bad dreams that invaded my sleep the first night grew in intensity each night after that. It appeared there was limited waiting time for the lineup of my dead ancestors. They came in droves to give me wisdom from the past. My pea brain could only digest small parts of their information.

I had an image of each ancestor's appearance from the stories my Grandma Lu and Grandma Wick had shared with me. Some apparitions came in traditional Indian dress and some, strange as it may sound, were dressed in modern clothes. Others came with the flesh melting from their faces and some dressed in tuxedos with top hats. This caused me to scream out in the middle of the night, which brought the wrath of the old man on my behind.

The most impressive image was old Uncle Yellow Robe with his dog-eared Holy Bible tucked under his arm. He had a light that emitted from a Masonic medal around his turkey-skin neck. I thought he might preach me a good sermon. But to my surprise, he wanted to tell me about the value of my gift.

I had the ability to communicate with the ancestors. Along with the ancient secrets of the lost medicines, this was only a small part of the knowledge I would gain. I had trouble wrapping my brain around the fact that my love of seeing ghosts was this great gift from God. Most of the time I didn't know if I was awake or asleep as I continued to see things while awake that just, to put it kindly, scared the flipping crap out of me!

I continued to press my Grandma Lu to tell me the rest of the story about Grandma Reed's life. She had gotten ticked off over my stupid suggestion to use the roots that I was guided to by the ghost of Grandma Reed as a hair control medicine. How would that work you ask? When you get your hair to the exact length you want, the root medicine will stop any further growth. This would allow you to do more important stuff, like run the streets with your boys instead of having to get a haircut. If the hair control drug worked, then we could take it to the next level of managing the growth of fingernails and toenails.

You can see why my Grandma Lu was so ticked at my demented thought process. Instead, I should have suggested making cures for a few serious diseases like cancer, heart problems or arthritis. As you can see, I am still not getting the greater picture of my God-given gift. But you must admit, the hair and nails drug could save a lot of wasted time and energy.

I guess some irony had to come my way sooner or later. I was now starting my freshman year at Rock Hill High School. As you might guess, our mascot was The Fighting Red Men. I didn't have a problem with that until Magoo said he would be angry if they were called The Fighting Black Men. That sure brought things into focus! I guess I should have been proud to be the only person with Indian blood on a team called The Fighting Red Men.

What really got me upset was the coach who scrimmaged our 90-pound weakling freshman squad against the varsity tough guys. Needless to say, they broke up our spindly bodies along with our will to play football. If any good came from this beat down, it was a return to my Grandma Lu's home with all her Indian remedies. And hopefully, her willingness to continue telling the stories about my Grandma Reed's life.

Yet again, I seem to have aggravated the world. According to my Grandma Lu, I can't keep a secret. She somehow doesn't comprehend the concept of what a trusted friend I have in Magoo. Lulu Golden blew her top when she learned that he knew all about our strange family secrets!

Apparently, the straw that broke the camel's back was my complaint about Grandma Lu's meat poultice (combined with stinky Indian roots) that she had once strapped to my body. I probably would not have complained about it had it not slid down my pant leg in front of all my classmates at school. How do teachers know you're about to poop out a fat-back poultice all over their classroom? Maybe by the smell of meat. No matter, I am now known as "jerky, dick-meat boy."

My Grandma Lu can't see this meat fallout as a tragedy. No, it was only another opportunity to learn how to tighten up her stinky poultice. Nonetheless, we're not on speaking terms. It may be years before I get the rest of this story. Knowing how strong willed she can be, I may never hear it.

Hobbled by my football injuries, I stood on the muddy riverbank watching the Ohio River rush west to meet the Old Man of Rivers, the mighty Mississippi. I meditated on the value of God (The Great Good Spirit) in my life and the seven significant rivers in Willow (Ciicothe) Reed's life. I believe I have developed a love for this great Ohio River that is now playing an increased role in molding my short life.

I have gained an appreciation for my Grandma Reed's life on her seven rivers, from her birth on the Maumee to the end of her life here on the Ohio. Her unwavering Christian faith did not change, even with all the bad things that white man had done to her. *I wonder about God's power, blessings, and the number of great rivers that will guide me in my life and dreams.*

I can't end this story without telling about the hill, the bike, and the hell I put myself through. On one cold December day, I decided to ride my raggedy bike down Dead Man's Hill without using the brakes. I almost killed myself. I can't entirely explain what went wrong with my philosophical thinking while standing on that riverbank only a few weeks before.

I broke ties with my Grandma Lu. My gang of dumb-asses was split apart. And if that was not enough, my family moved further into the boondocks on Dog Fork Road! The most tragic part of this was that my Grandma Lu did not want to tell me the remainder of the story.

My grandma became extremely upset because I couldn't tell her who Ponce de Leon was and something about his hunting for the fountain of youth. I guess I flunked her history exam. While holding her precious bloodroot, Grandma Lu tried to explain to me how **it** was the object that old Ponce de Leon had been looking for in 1513 while traipsing through the swamps of Florida. Heck, the way she talked, Grandma Wick could have been my Grandma Reed at one hundred sixty-three years old!

All of these things combined made me decide to get on my rickety bike and ride. I thought I would lose my nerve when a car rounded the hairpin curve and almost hit me. I started to get off the bike and walk it down the hill, but I didn't. I was on my way down, and there was no way to turn back now! *This reminds me of my exit off the rim of the old sand pit.*

I realized I had no brakes, I couldn't stop! I decided that I would crash into the hillside of the road. With a quick glance, I changed my mind. I saw my Grandma Ciicothe Reed's ghost come running full speed from the rim of the woods with a tomahawk in her hand! *That's it! My wild imagination decided my fate, I was going to ride it out!* I felt that if I could make it, I would be a legend.

As I rounded the last hairpin curve, I was taken by surprise. The bike lurched forward, and the front wheel went rolling off. The forks impaled the pavement, and I was launched like a grenade over the handlebars into a steep ravine. I probably should have had a prayer or two in mind, but the only thought I had was that this legend was coming to an end!

EPILOGUE
The Ghost of Time

History can be a fog of memories by the people that lived it. Some people recorded an event shortly after it ended by using their own eyewitness accounts. Other people that witness the same event have accounts of that historical event that differ, sometimes completely. History is seldom recorded by the losers.

I don't like classifying the native peoples of this country as losers, but that is for each individual to decide for themselves. If you focus on what was lost by white man's greed, one might conclude that America was the loser. The Indian peoples' history was passed down from generation to generation through storytelling for thousands of years. The ghost of time consumed my spirit while telling this story, much of which came to me from my grandma's fog of memories as well as in my dreams and nightmares.

Ciicothe's journey and her life on these seven rivers are emblematic of the thousands of native people who, for what unknown reason, were separated from their families and tribes. Yet some Native Americans, through their will to survive, integrated into the white man's world. Some with remarkable success.

Some white people have no idea that they have Indian blood running through their veins. There are some who never want to know. Some may even have a father such as mine, who did everything within his power to berate our Indian heritage. Hopefully, you are as blessed as I was to have two grandmas to remember their history and share it with you before the ghost of time gets hungry and time on this earth runs short.

History was kind to some of this country's presidents, who in the native peoples' eyes were the equivalent of Adolph Hitler. This is a difficult concept for most people of this country to accept. However, it is a fact that some leaders believed in slavery, genocide, and the removal of the native people from their homelands. These same leaders founded our nation on greed and believed in a philosophy of keeping poor people fighting to kill other poor people. This greed theory lives on today to serve the needs of the wealthy, and the power-hungry people.

Did Willow Ciicothe Reed's journey from Tippecanoe to South Point on the Ohio leave you wanting to know the rest of her story? Then be prepared to read the continuation of family secrets, ghosts, and skeletons in the closet in *Ciicothe's Brothers Reed*.